The Growing and Giant Woman Collection:

Volume 5

By: Amber Collins

Lab Partners

Nick had been in community college for what felt like fifty years, but in truth it was only six. He'd hopped majors three times, had lost financial aid twice, and now that he had his head on straight, he was poised to graduate with an RBA—a reagents bachelor of arts—what his mom jokingly called a 'major in nothing.' She wasn't completely wrong—it was simply a conglomerate of course hours that the college lumped into a program so that the average waffler could graduate. Without pursuing a master's degree, it was rather useless, but he decided to take things one step at a time. And the next step: Passing his Earth science class.

The class itself wasn't so bad—it was the lab portion that got to him. He hated the hands-on science stuff and wished he could just take a test and be done. But no, the class was geared toward fresh out of high school kids, something he was not, and this new way of teaching ran counter to his way of learning. So, the professor—a large, beefy man named Hendricks, had assigned them all a final project, an experiment on par with middle school kids. It felt incredibly silly, but he didn't have much of a choice.

What made this assignment even more difficult was that the professor didn't allow an individual project. He was forcing the twenty-four students in his class to partner up and together complete a project. This wouldn't have been so bad, but he was late the day that they drew names out of a hat, and by default he ended up with the last person chosen.

Beth Anderson.

Beth was called the Homicidal Giantess on campus. The homicidal part was probably undeserving, but the giantess part was all true. She was pushing eight feet tall, had held many track and basketball records in high school.

She couldn't even fit through the doors because of her size, not to mention her wide chest and hips. But the way she acquired the homicidal part of her nickname was what troubled Nick.

She'd taken three biology classes throughout college—one in every other semester—and each time her lab partner had mysteriously vanished. No one spoke it, of course not to her, but it was a little off-putting when Nick thought about it. Billy Kramer, Eddie Matthews, and Rick Henson. All three of them, simply gone one day. No one ever linked them to Beth, but the students on campus whispered about her—and when Hendricks announced that Nick would be her partner, potentially placing him as number four on her hit list, the whole class seemed to hush, as if out of respect for his soon to be missing status.

The students had lots of crazy ideas where Beth was concerned. Some said she used acid to melt them in the bathtub, and that she kept their tooth fillings as souvenirs. Others said she cut them up and ate them like some kind of cannibalistic psycho. Nick wasn't really worried about any of that, nor did he feed into it. He simply wanted this project behind him so he could graduate and start the next leg of his journey.

After class, he sat in the parking lot in his car and sent Beth a text message. He'd gotten her number from the class sign-up board in the hallway outside the classroom. She was rather pleasant to talk to, and he couldn't imagine any of the bad stuff being true, especially since it was farfetched. She had a great idea to do a rather simple project on storm clouds using cotton balls and water. The more she talked, the more he understood that she was going to be doing the bulk of this project. He wasn't a science guy, and she clearly had a good idea of what she wanted to do. Maybe he could just sit back and watch and let her do all the heavy lifting, the same way he coasted back in high school. At the end of their conversation, he agreed to come by her place that evening for dinner and to begin working on the project.

She lived in an apartment within sight of the college, between a drugstore and a yoga studio. When she opened the door, she had to crane her head to the side to see him, her mess of red hair falling down past her shoulders. Beth was a pretty girl, and although Nick loved tall women, he found her to be incredibly intimidating. She was a beast—her arms corded with muscles, her breasts like a pair of watermelons, and her ass like saddlebags that she carried everywhere she went. Even her calves were decked out in muscles. He wondered if she were naturally fit or if this was part of her condition—for surely there *had* to be a condition—that made her so big. When she was standing straight, she couldn't even see him without looking down between her breasts.

"Come on in, small stuff," she said, and then in a voice somewhat sympathetic. "Sorry, that was probably mean. Come on in, Nick."

Her apartment was nice, sparsely decorated as if to accommodate her size. She had been in the middle of watching television, but something smelled good in the kitchen. He took his shoes off and followed her through the open space and found her working at the counter, stirring a pot of what he discovered was spaghetti sauce.

"My mom's recipe," she said. "I hope you're hungry. I'm incapable of making spaghetti for less than a hundred people."

He grinned, then laughed, completely put at ease by this seemingly gentle giant. A part of him immediately felt bad for assuming she were capable of anything bad. Her whole life had probably been a train wreck of misconceptions.

Nick seated himself at her table while she finished up their plates, and he couldn't tear his eyes away from her ass. It was bouncing up and down with each step she took. He was mesmerized by its rhythm, and she almost caught him staring as she whirled around with two steaming helpings of spaghetti. Luckily, he was quick to avert his eyes and begin unrolling his napkin to place in his lap.

Beth turned out to be a great cook, as Nick quickly realized once he'd taken a bite of her delicious spaghetti. At first, they didn't talk much, only stuffed their faces, but soon it became rather awkward and he didn't want to pass the time away in utter silence. He was here to get a passing grade, after all.

"So I guess I'm your punishment, huh?" said Beth, swirling spaghetti onto her fork.

"What?" he said in mid-bite.

"You were late for class the day we were being assigned partners. You definitely weren't lucky."

"Why do you say that? Are you going to get us a bad grade?" he said, but he knew what she was referencing. For all intents and purposes, Beth was actually a good student.

"I'll get us a good grade, but you know what I mean."

"I don't listen to rumors," he quickly countered. "I'm just here to do a project so I can graduate. Tell me about this thing. Clouds, huh?"

They finished their meal while Beth animatedly talked about storm clouds. She was a real science buff, but Nick couldn't follow along. The more she talked the more he could see that she possessed an uncommon intelligence, and was quite interested in physical science. He smiled when appropriate and agreed to all her points, but he mostly just listened. This girl was talking way over his head.

After they ate, he helped her clean up, even though she insisted he didn't. Standing next to her was rather odd from Nick's spot at the ground—he was only five feet tall, so this goddess's shadow fell across him wherever he went. Every now and then, he would turn around while wiping down counters or returning something to the fridge, and come faced with her enormous breasts. If she were close, he couldn't eve see her head because they came out so far from her body.

When it was time to get started on the work, she showed him to a den located off the kitchen. It had a coffee table dominating the center of the room, and upon it her laptop, a jar of cotton balls, and a few poster boards that they would assemble to create a diorama for their project.

She guided him toward his seat and once more he was overcome by her sheer size. The ass, passing by him, was so close to his face that he wanted to lean over and kiss it, bite it, or at least slap it. There was a stirring in his pants, and he couldn't help but feel overcome by her sexuality. Her scent was driving him crazy and he wondered if she realized the affect she had on men—or at the very least, *this* man.

While she was reaching across the table to grab a gluestick, her breasts touched the table and pressed them wide. Nick averted his eyes, but this time he was too slow, as he'd dawdled far too long, fantasizing about the crack between her cleavage. He wondered what her nipples looked like, how they felt, how they would taste in his mouth. Subconsciously he licked his lips, but she was able to quickly make the connection, and she sat back and started laughing, her breasts rising and falling with each chuckle.

"What?" he asked, trying to downplay what had happened but knowing the reddening of his face was giving him away.

"Don't say what, little man. You know." He dared a glance up at her, and she was squeezing her breasts together, making them appear even larger. "Do you like them?"

"Um. . ."

"Um is not an answer. Do you like them or not?" She let them go and rested them on the table. He couldn't keep from casting them a sidelong glance.

"They're nice," he said finally.

She grew quiet for a moment, as if she didn't expect him to fully admit it. Then, she said, "Do you want to see them?"

His face, if possible, had grown even redder, and he looked down at his clipboard as he felt a rush of heat on his cheeks. But something in the way she said it made him think it was okay, that she would truly humor him. Nick was single. Beth appeared to be single. What's the worst that could happen?

"Yeah, actually I would," he said, pulling confidence up from nowhere. He leaned back in his chair and folded his arms over.

She grinned and sat up straight, then pulled her shirt up from the bottom, then snapped it over her neck until she was sitting there in only a black, lacy bra that was struggling to keep her melons up and tucked in. When she unclasped the front, he wasn't ready for such large breasts to spill out and bounce in place. It was almost like an optical illusion, and their weight held them down almost past the table. She lifted them, running fingers across her nipples until they started to stand at attention. Beth never took her eyes off Nick, careful to watch his expression. With each flick of her fingers, the nipples grew harder and longer until they were like little daggers. The areolas were dark, the size of saucers.

"Well say something, silly," she said, taking turns bobbing them up and down. Their weight looked incredible.

"I like them. Very nice," he said. At this point, he was rock hard beneath the table, and he fought the urge to reach down and give it a stroke through his shorts.

"Do you wanna touch them?" He flashed her a wide-eyed look that said he didn't believe what he was hearing, so she elaborated. "It's okay. I'll let you." She turned her chair so that she was facing him more directly.

He reached out a shaky hand and touched first above her left breast, and then, as her hands moved aside, dragged his fingers down to fondle her nipple. She was smiling, showing a lot of teeth when she bit her bottom lip. The nipple became even more firm in his fingers and he could see her skin break out in goosebumps. Nick moved to the other one, and with each touch it was like she was jolted by electricity. Her mouth hung open as she watched him work, and then, she said something he wasn't expecting.

"Suck them."

"What? Really?" he confirmed, already moving forward.

"Yeah. Do it," she said.

He wasted no time leaning in, taking her right nipple and popping it into his mouth. She was so warm, and tasted so good. Her little moans were driving him wild and he found his hands reaching below to stroke his own dick through the shorts. She leaned right back into him, but she took his hand away and replaced it with her own much bigger and stronger one. His eyes were about to roll back into his head just from being touched, so he increased his sucking, his licking, his kissing. His warm breath rolled across her flesh and made her tingle.

They kissed for a few minutes, but he had to stand up to even get across her breasts. He loved how they were pressed against his chest, and her tongue fought his for supremacy. He put his hands in her hair and pulled, to which she elicited a satisfied moan, and then returned the favor by pulling his back and kissing down his chest, as she undid the buttons.

"Can we go to the bedroom?" she asked, stopping and resting her hands on his shorts. He wanted to pull his dick out right then and there and let her suck it.

"Yeah, let's go," he said, following her out of the den and up a short flight of steps to a massive bedroom with a California King sized bed. It looked custom made, surely had to be since she was so large. Either that or she slept diagonally.

They crashed on the bed, the wooden frame creaking under their combined weight. She threw him down and aggressively ripped off his shirt and then his pants. When she saw his dick, she made a little moan, as most women did. Nick was short, but he made up for it in one very specific, very useful spot.

"My, my," said Beth, leaning over and dragging her tongue across his shaft. "He's quite big. Eight inches?"

"Nine," Nick corrected.

"You might just do some damage with this," she said.

"That's the idea," he said, and then was lost to pleasure as she took him fully in her mouth.

Not many girls could rest their lips on his stomach as his dick normally gagged all but those with the least reflex. But Beth was sucking him with such fervor that he was grabbing at her hair, letting it sift through his fingers during the gentle moments, and snatching tight handfuls when she was aggressive. When she looked up at him with her large, green eyes, he thought he would explode right then and there, but Nick was good at riding the edge, so to speak, so he made sure to fight her rhythm with just enough effort to keep himself in the game.

She pulled back and stroked him for a moment, licking her lips. There was something in the way she eyed him. He couldn't quite put his finger on it, but it was almost as though she were sizing him up, wondering what her big body could do with his smaller one.

"I have a confession," she said. "Something I don't talk about a lot, but I'm really comfy with you."

"What is it?" he asked, sitting up on his elbows. He'd listen to anything, so long as she kept stroking his dick.

"I have a lot of trouble getting off. I've only had like one orgasm in my whole life."

"No way!" he said. "Are you serious?"

"Yep. But it's okay. I'm used to it. I just like to warn guys because some of you get really offended when it doesn't happen."

"It's cool with me, as long as you're having fun."

"That's the idea," she said, mirroring his earlier words. She sat back on her ass and threw her legs into the air, then pulled down her shorts and panties. Beth had a beautiful shaved pussy, and her stomach was so toned that he could see the muscles ripple beneath her skin whenever she made a minor movement.

She pushed him back completely flat and then walked her knees up around his body. She looked simply massive from this angle, as if her head rose to the ceiling. Beth was smiling at him, but he only saw the center of her mouth, as her breasts blotted out the woman above them. His attention was refocused when she grabbed his cock and helped guide it into her waiting pussy. She was already so wet, so warm, and surprisingly, so tight.

"Oh, damn," she said, her words ending in a long, drawn out moan. "I haven't felt like this in a long time!"

She started riding him, the force of her body slightly painful on his legs. She leaned down, but she was so large that her breasts fell right on his face and her arms moved behind his head, to grip the posts of the bed. Her hips were gyrating out, moving in circles, and he could already feel her wetness. One of her hands disappeared below and started rubbing circles around her clit. After that, she was nearly gushing, and if this wasn't an orgasm, he didn't know what it could be.

"You're gonna do it," she said excitedly. "You're gonna get me off! Oh damn, not good, not good!"

Not good? he wondered. Nick didn't know what to make of that, but before he had time to ponder it, his body was drenched in her juices and she rolled aside, panting heavily.

"That was amazing," said Nick, although he didn't get off.

"Yeah," she said, holding up a hand to her face as if she were just now seeing it. He hoped she didn't start acting all weird now that they'd had sex.

"I need to use your bathroom," he said, noticing the sink in the room at the foot of the bed.

"I have another confession," she said to his back, softly.

"Okay, just give me a minute, okay?" He turned and shut the door.

Nick did his business, and while he was sitting there, he could've sworn he heard gentle moans coming from the bedroom. Apparently one big O wasn't enough for her, so she was rubbing another out on her own. He smiled at the thought, and was somewhat proud that he was the first guy to make her cum. Nick flushed, stood to walk out, then ripped open the door, intent on having another go at her—

—but came faced against a pussy as large as his whole head. There was nothing on the other side of the door but legs and feet, and he slowly looked up, expecting to see the giantess smiling down at him, but her breasts had grown disproportionate to her body, and now obscured every inch of her face. He took a step back, and she went down to a knee so she could better see him. Now, she didn't even look like a person—now she looked like a monster, but a sexy monster with the biggest breasts and ass he'd ever seen. When she was able to fix him with her giant, green eyes, he relaxed a little. Beth had a very disarming look to her.

"About that confession . . .," she said, voice trailing off. She returned to the bed, putting her massive ass in his face. He fought the urge to reach out and slap it because he could tell she was being serious for a moment, so he followed her out into the bedroom. Currently, Beth was around twelve feet tall, her neck turned uncomfortably to the side. She sat on the bed, the frame bowing painfully. Nick risked a seat next to her.

"I've trained myself not to get off," she said. "I've had orgasms on my own. I used to be four feet and nine inches tall. And then I came, and I came again. And I lived as an eight-foot giantess for many years. Guess this is my new size now." She looked up at her ceilings, as if seeing them for the first time ever.

"I'm sorry," he said. "I should've stopped."

"No," she said, then leaned down and kissed him. It was odd because her tongue was so large. "I enjoyed it. And I'm enjoying this new size!" She stood up and did a twirl, and this time he smacked her ass when it was facing him.

"I bet you wouldn't feel my dick now," he said, stroking it.

"Oh honey, that sounds like a challenge. Besides, I need to get *you* off."

"Yes you do."

She wasted no time moving into the floor, her knees coming down on the carpet with a muffled boom. Her giant hands rested on his chest, her nails beautifully manicured, and then pushed him back. Now, her mouth worked him like a vacuum, easily swallowing his cock, but then again it was no bigger than a few inches to her.

"Gonna cum for me?" she asked, her warm breath feeling nice against his skin.

"It's looking that way," he said, and a moment later he knew for sure. His legs were shaking as his fingers wrapped into her hair again, this time feeling much different. And then he blew his load, her mouth quickly and easily licking him clean. His dick was still red and throbbing when she pulled him from her mouth.

After that, she took control, pulling him up to the headboard even before his dick had gone soft. It wouldn't be in such a state long because Beth was just getting started. She brought her knees up around him, put her hands flat against the wall, then shoved her pussy right into his face. She was still incredibly wet, her scent and taste wonderful. Beth arched her back and started to grind into him, rubbing her slit up and down until her clit was able to be caught up in the process.

Each time she moved, the bed squeaked because they were hopping it back and forth across the floor. Nick wasn't in control of the situation, so he only put out his tongue and attempted to lick the giantess as she moved by. This was Beth's playtime, and she was having it however she wanted. But when he started to feel her juices seep down his chest, he grew concerned. Should she be doing this?

"Beth," he said between breaths. "Beth, stop. You're gonna grow again!"

Hearing him say it was enough to snap her from her reverie, so she slowed down, then moved away, leaving him dripping wet. She had a defeated look on her face, and he could tell she was disappointed. That had to be a terrible way to live—to only edge close to orgasm without ever going over. Nick didn't think he possessed that kind of willpower—he was used to jerking off at least once a day.

"Wanna stay over?" she asked him suddenly.

"Sure," he said. He was still feeling a little bad for making her grow again.

"I won't eat you," she said. "Promise."

***

The next morning he woke up to the sound of the trash truck banging cans. He sat up, and yesterday's antics came flooding back. Their sex had been magical, but curling up to her during the night to fall asleep was even better. She pulled him close and he drifted away in the crook of her arm, surrounded by her giant breasts. But now, she was nowhere to be found. Perhaps she was out, strolling down the street completely naked.

He threw on his clothes and walked downstairs, but Beth was nowhere to be found. Nick had assumed she'd gone downstairs to fix breakfast, but the kitchen was just as spotless and immaculate as they'd left it the night before. He called her name a few times, but she didn't answer. But . . . he did see the backdoor standing open, the one that led out to the fenced-in yard.

Outside, it was starting to drizzle, and just when he heard a loud boom to his right, he looked down into the grass and saw a footprint—only this one didn't belong to a twelve-foot woman. This one . . .

"Hey short stuff."

. . . belonged to a *twenty*-foot woman.

He turned to look up at her, but just as he couldn't see her face when she was eight feet and twelve feet, he certainly couldn't now, when her breasts were so far out of his reach. Her nipples were too big to wrap his hands around now, and just yesterday they still fit in his mouth. Beth put a hand on her hip and locked her leg. The sheer weight of her was making her feet sink into the ground.

"What did you do?" he asked, but knew that was a silly question.

"Sorry," she said. "But after you got me off it . . . made me want more. I tried to be good. I really did! But you know, one thing led to another and I started fingering myself. And when I got off, I quickly ran outside. What do you think of me?" She did another twirl, her ass bouncing past. And then, as if remembering he had a fondness for it, she bent low and put it right in his face. Nick reached a hand up and stroked it, knowing her body was far too large now to give any sort of pleasure . . . but she was going to try anyway.

Beth sat down in the grass and spread her legs. Nick was hesitant, surely not wanting to get her worked up because what would her next size even be? Thirty feet tall? Fifty? One-hundred? But as he stood there, watching her pink insides pulse, feeling her heat, tasting her scent on the air, he knew he couldn't pass up this opportunity. Her pussy could take his whole leg right now, and he wanted to try that very thing.

Nick approached, dragging his fingers across her thigh, to which she broke out in goosebumps and lifted her heels off the ground. She settled, relaxed, and watched as he came toward her. Beth had to hold her massive breasts aside so that she could see him. When he reached her most wonderful spot, he took a knee, then sat on his ass. He pulled his shorts off and then, carefully eased a foot inside her. She recoiled, but only because such a thing was surprising at first. Once more, she settled, and let him continue.

She was tight, but then again, he was pushing a leg into her. Beth relaxed a little, giving him clearance to keep pushing. Her whole body was threatening to upend, to start bucking, but she made the conscious effort to keep her bottom on the grass. When Nick's whole leg disappeared, he started to rotate at the ankle, and that's when she started to howl—her hands reaching up into her hair. The more she moved side to side, the more he worried about her snapping his leg. Currently, she was driving herself down, deeper into the ground. Whenever she finally did stand, there would probably be a five-foot divot in the dirt.

Nick pulled his leg out quickly, to which she made a little yelp and then stared at him expectantly, wondering if he was going to continue some other way. He got down on his knees and used her thighs as support, and then pushed his face right into her. It was quite the job licking her, starting at the bottom and riding her lips up to her clit. If not for her wetness his mouth would've dried up on the first pass.

"I've got another confession," she said somewhere above him.

"Geez, now what?" he asked, but didn't even stop to wipe his chin. He kept on servicing her.

"My lab partners. They all did what you're doing and um, well . . . I sort of kept them."

He looked up to see if she were kidding but couldn't see her face. The tone in her voice suggested that she wasn't.

"What do you mean?" he asked, feeling his body go cold.

"They're down in my basement. Don't worry! I take good care of them. And I'll take good care of you too. My growth will wear off eventually, and then we can play this whole game all over again."

He wanted to object, to say something, to run off, but she put a firm hand behind his head and continued to thrust her hips, rubbing her pussy and up and down his face. And then, she let go, and her juices lashed out and threatened to drown him. She relaxed her hold for just a moment so that he could get out of the way, perhaps to keep his lungs from filling with her juices, but after that, her whole body was trembling, and he knew what was coming.

First his head disappeared inside her, and then his shoulders. She was growing, much quicker than before. The walls of her pussy were all around him as her ever-increasing fingers wrapped around his body and pushed him in. And then, before he knew what was happening, his entire body was inside, meaning he was no more than a human sex toy for her. How big did that make her? Fifty feet? His mind couldn't wrap around it, but he knew he needed to get out.

But that presented a new problem.

Every time he moved, he could feel her tense up, the muscles contracting to hold him in place. It took a few tries to realize that his movements were turning her on. And now Nick was left with a dilemma—stay inside the giantess and suffocate, or attempt to get out and possibly get her off again, thus making her even bigger. Nick decided to try the latter, and when he grabbed at her lips and pushed his head out, her juices finished the job, and he was expelled halfway across the lawn.

He looked back at her, now blotting out the house behind her. She threw her head back and laughed. Nick didn't even try to run away—he knew she'd catch him. Instead, he sat down, resigned himself to his fate, and watched as her body began to swell in all directions . . .

The
Goliath Virus

October 7th, 2020

We have officially been quarantined since the first of the month. I was told by my agency, *The Williamson Journal*, to begin chronicling the virus, compiling a journal that will later be the basis for a story. While neither me nor Ashleigh have shown any signs of contracting the Goliath Virus (or GOLIATH-20 if you want to get technical), we've still chosen to do the right thing, which the news loves to coin 'social distancing.' I feel fine. Ashleigh feels fine. We're just going to watch the world from the safety of our apartment and see how this all plays out. So far, there isn't any panic, no anarchy, even if people's first choice is to buy up all the gasoline and toilet paper.

The news can be rather upsetting. I can remember when the story first broke. The virus originated in the United States, in California to be exact. There's so much strange shit over there, in the land of make-believe, that no one really batted an eye when patient zero, a woman named Molly Hamilton, suddenly started to grow. Molly had been a crossing guard for an elementary school, and she didn't even notice she'd changed until she was on day three, and already close to ten feet tall. She became a national news story, but she didn't remain one for long. Only a day later did others come forward, also exhibiting changes in size.

It started in California but it didn't end there. In two weeks there were cases all across the United States. In a month it was in almost every country. And as of last week, it was estimated that 92% of all women had it. The CDC and WHO quickly surmised this was some sort of virus, and that it was passed only between women who were at least twenty years old. Men weren't affected at all, not directly anyway. We'd seen reports of domestic abuse cases on the news, how battered women who'd lived life cowering in their apartments were suddenly able to turn the tables and beat (and in at least two cases kill) their abusers. The world had flipped upside down, and I'm glad we are able to stay indoors.

We are as prepared for it as possible. Ashleigh and I went to the thrift store in town on Saturday to pick up some oversized clothes. Shoes, belts, pants, and tops that would all give us a little bit of 'growing' room should we need it. Goliath was trending on all social networking, and it was becoming fashionable to show off your new body in baggy clothes.

"Samantha has it," said Ashleigh from her computer chair. She turned her phone around to show me a picture of a girl showing several pictures of her baggy clothes and, on a few occasions, the tight ones. "She's gained a whole foot by now. I'm freaking out here,."

"It's going to be fine," I say, but I don't really know that.

My name is Hannah, and I'll be your guide for this adventure.

October 9th, 2020

Ashleigh woke up with a sore throat and she's been sneezing her head off. Those are the first symptoms but we are being optimistic—it's October, the leaves are falling, the pollen is all stirred up. I'm holding to allergies. I feel fine so far, so that's a plus. It's been over a week since either of us have been out of the apartment, and seeing as how the symptoms start to appear after three or four days, I'm not so sure how either of us could catch it. Ashleigh hasn't even been out in two weeks. She also works for *The Williamson Journal*, but she manages the website and is able to work from home even when the world isn't under quarantine.

It wasn't all bad. We were getting to spend a lot of quality time together, watching television shows that we'd put off because we were so busy. Ashleigh was already preparing for the change, as she never took of her comfy clothes. She never wore socks—neither of us did. We simply lounged around the apartment in whatever felt the best.

I walked into the bedroom this morning and she had her art supplies all across the floor. Her long, red hair was cascading down her pale skin. She was getting bored— Ashleigh wasn't much of a reader like me. I could be content indoors from now until eternity. To her, life was all about video games and Netflix and painting. Currently she was turning her footprints into butterflies by stepping in paint, then stepping onto the canvas. After it dried she painted the antennae and legs to complete the picture.

"How are you feeling?" I asked. It was a very honest question, but I was also combing for info—I was desperate to see if she were still symptomatic.

"Just tired," she said, stating the next symptom after sore throat and sneeze. "And my feet . . . they're tingly." And there was number four.

"Try to get some rest, okay?"

For the rest of the night I sat in front of the television. There was no shortage of news coverage on the Goliath pandemic. Everywhere you looked, women were sprouting up, inching bigger and bigger. Many were quarantined, but even more were not. The president tried to shut down the economy by issuing a national Stay-At-Home order, but for many—mainly service and medical

personnel—this wasn't an option. So the news showed
several nurses wearing undersized scrubs, faces covered in
masks, still tending to patients. They couldn't even fit
shoes, so they tied plastic bags around their ankles. I wrote
about these ladies, as well as those I saw in the service
business.

Waitresses—the ones who served at restaurants that
refused to shut down—waited tables while wearing masks,
their skirts riding so high that people could see under them.
Modesty seemed to go right out the window with the
introduction of Goliath, and I loved it more than I would
care to admit.

October 10th, 2020

I woke up sneezing this morning. Normally, I'd
play it off as a simple cold since I didn't suffer from
allergies, but the moment I turned the television on, the first
news story to break today did little to alleviate me. In big,
flashing letters across the bottom of the screen, it read:
CONFIRMED: WOMEN CAN CARRY THE VIRUS
WITHOUT ANY SYMPTOMS FOR UP TO THREE
WEEKS.

The woman reporting this—Suzanne Martel—one
of the most well-known reporters in the city, was clearly
infected. The way she hunched her arms in a suit jacket that
was too small for her told me that she'd only had this
growth spurt in the last few hours. But in the middle of her
delivery, she reared her head back and sneezed, to which
the entire studio fell quiet, her co-anchor included. And
finally, as if resigning herself to what was to come,
Suzanne sat back in her chair, tossed her pen onto the desk,

then pulled her feet up. The entire country was looking at the soles of her feet.

"These have been tingling all day. And they're going to get much bigger, don't you think?" After that, the program went off, replaced by the rainbow bars and an awful drone.

My blood went cold at the thought of her story, and perhaps it was just in my mind, but my throat started to hurt. When I stood up, the soles of my feet were tingling, and as I walked, the sensitivity was driving me crazy. I had to stop every few feet and I hoped Ashleigh wouldn't see me. Every so often I had to pull one foot on top of the other, massage, and then keep moving.

This morning had already started off on a low note, but it was nothing compared to when I opened the door to the office and walked in, only to see Ashleigh on the floor, crying. She had paint all over her feet again, a bright blue. And she was making more butterflies.

"What's wrong, babe?" I asked her, putting my lips to her neck. She was so warm—fevered even. At this point, I should have stopped trying to assume it was anything *but* the virus.

"Look," she said, and showed me her latest artwork, a blue-soled butterfly with antennae drawn on with thick, black strokes.

"Okay? What's wrong?"

She pulled out another one, this one in red paint, and already dried. It was slightly crumpled at the corner.

"This is the one I did the day we were first quarantined." She held them up side-by-side.

I gasped.

The blue one she'd done today was noticeably bigger. Still, I tried to downplay her fears.

"Maybe it's just the way the paint dried."

"It's not, Hannah," said Ashleigh, sniffing back tears. She pulled out a ruler. "I measured. I wear a size nine. I have an eleven-inch foot right now!" She collapsed into my arms and I stroked her head while blowing a strand of my own blond hair out of my eyes. We would get through this. And I would write all about it while we did.

"I want a pretty picture too," I said, rubbing a hand across my sole.

"You do?"

"Yeah, make me a butterfly. It'll be fun."

It took her mind off of things and for that, I was glad. I dipped my feet in white paint and stamped them on the paper. We sat watching it dry for a long time before she got up and started to clean her brushes.

She came back hobbling and I asked what's wrong. "My feet . . . they're still so sensitive and tingly."

"Yeah," I agreed, reaching down and rubbing mine, even though they were covered in paint. "Mine are too."

"It's really weird, like we aren't getting enough blood flow or something. The way they go to sleep like we're on a long car ride."

"It's very weird," I agreed. "But hey, looks like we have something in common, huh?"

She was in good spirits the rest of the day, as we'd bought our quarantine food and stocked up on all her favorite staples. But as she sat at the kitchen nook, working on her laptop and eating a grilled cheese sandwich, I couldn't help but notice how her legs looked a little longer, how, as she scrunched her toes, they were thicker. She'd painted her toes a bright blue a couple of mornings ago, and now, ever so subtly, there was a natural frame around them—her feet had grown slightly bigger and now the polish had become a bordered square in the center of her nails.

We played *Scrabble* before bed, and to take her mind off things, we added a rule that always made her smile. For every ten-point word someone played, the other person had to take off an article of clothing. Ashleigh was far more open about her body than me, and as luck would have it, I found myself losing to her every time. Her body was a little on the chubby side while I was lanky, but the game revealed all, nonetheless. But it was a nice change of pace and it got us both naked just in time to go to sleep.

I suppose that if my story is to make sense, you, the reader, need a few key details spelled out up front. I'm a naturally tall girl, no Goliath tampering needed. I stand at a commanding five feet and eleven inches. My girlfriend (for she is my other half if you haven't guessed by now) is much shorter, coming up to my chin. Ashleigh is a mere five feet and three inches tall. Or at least she was when I kissed her forehead the morning before we made the discovery.

Before I turned off my lamp, I leaned in to kiss her, and I didn't have to stoop nearly as much as I normally did. She'd gained a few inches throughout the day. And although she wasn't as tall as me (yet), there was clearly a noticeable change. Her eyes were welling with tears and I did my best to quell them. There was no use in getting upset.

We went to bed and I wrapped my arm around her. She was shaking. Ashleigh didn't deal well with any sort of stress. I was the more level-headed one, seeing the bigger picture and coming up with a plan. But I knew I needed to calm her down, to make her fall asleep so we could together see what tomorrow brought. Slowly, my hand descended, my fingers shoving into her panties. I thought she'd fight me, but her body relaxed.

My fingers went to work, finding her sweet spot, reading her body language. Ashleigh was an easy girl to get off, much different than me, but I often used toys and my added size advantage when it came to pleasing her. She was incredibly wet after just a few minutes, and it was clear that part of her stress had been pent-up sexual frustration. With everything going on, between the virus and trying to figure out a work-from-home routine, we didn't have much time for such pleasures. But now, life was slowing down for a moment, and with it I could feel her stress flood away. When she finally did get off, she wrapped her hands around my arm, still shaking, and finally relaxed, her breathing coming out ragged.

Sleep was one of the good things about the virus—it only activated when you were awake, meaning so far anyone who'd been positive with GOLIATH-20 woke up roughly the same size as when they went to bed. But still, it was a new virus, a radical body-altering bug, and new data were being reported every day. When I finally did go to sleep, Ashleigh was already snoring lightly. Today was a good day. I hoped the morning would bring good news.

October 11th, 2020

The morning did not bring good news.

I woke up to Ashleigh measuring herself on the bathroom doorframe. She had a magic marker and was slashing a line across her head. Then, she took a tape measure and added up the inches so that she could notate that to the side. Currently she was sixty-seven inches—meaning she'd grown four inches tall during this ordeal.

I fixed her breakfast while watching her drag her art supplies from the bedroom back into the office. With coffee cup in hand, I entered the small room and found laying out a sheet of chart paper on the floor. It was a big sheet, around three-feet by two-feet, and we used them at work to storyboard our articles. But now, she was laying it flat so she could stand on it. Then, she used a pencil to trace her foot.

"Come in here," said Ashleigh when she was done. She pulled out another piece of chart paper and laid it next to the one that now had the outline of her foot. "I want to start one for you too."

"Okay," I said gently. This was how she worked through stress—she recorded data. To see her work on the *Journal's* website was amazing, as she could list stats from the last five years with great detail.

After I stood on the paper and allowed her to trace my feet (noticing that I needed a pedicure, stat), she recorded the data along the side. She'd made me stand at the left side of the chart, and I knew why—she expected us both to get much bigger and she wanted to show a progression.

"My feet are twelve inches now," she said. "Three inches bigger than normal. Yours are still a ten, so you don't seem to be infected." Ashleigh, for such a short girl, had naturally large feet. But now, they were literally a foot long.

We attempted to relax with yoga. It worked better for me than it did her, but at least I could lead by example and show her that it was possible to remain calm in such a difficult time. It felt nice to stretch, to feel the muscles in my back align, to feel my calves and shoulders loosen.

"How big do you think you'll be by tomorrow?" I asked her, wondering if it was a good idea.

"I don't know. Maybe I'll get another foot taller?" Her eyes were closed, her arms up in the air above her head. "And you?"

"Well obviously I'm going to be at least twenty-feet tall," I said, sounding silly but hoping it didn't rattle her. She simply breathed through her nose and kept right along with her pose. Yoga had been a good idea.

Later that evening, we watched more of the news. It was required for me because I had a ZOOM meeting tomorrow, and we were reporting on so many things. The virus data seemed to change almost every five minutes, and it took every ounce of my journalistic integrity to keep ahead of the curve. Tonight, the main focus was how many clothing companies had stepped up to make garments for the 'Supersized' ladies. A college girls' basketball team in Tampa had all tested positive for the virus, and were in various sizes. Their school had made them new jerseys. The girls weren't practicing social distancing, which was apparent by their group photo. The segment ended showing the team of infected girls playing another team of infected girls. Each one wore baggy shorts and shirts, and every single female was barefoot. I wondered how they got past regulations for such a game.

On the television was Suzanne Martel, one of the most famous giantesses currently working. She was reporting from her home now, in quarantine, and she was wearing baggy clothes that helped hide her mass. She was in good spirits and people loved to listen to her because she'd become a public figure on how to deal with the changes. She gave women hope, and for that, I was grateful.

One bit of good news did come tonight—the virus was making everyone grow double. Meaning if you were a six-foot woman, you'd wind up twelve feet tall. This hadn't been properly confirmed, but there were enough cases to suggest it. That was a relief because until now, there was panic that women would just continue to grow and grow, possibly throwing our whole planet off its rotation.

"You know you're going to get it, right?" said Ashleigh. By now, she was creeping up close to my own size.

"Probably," I said, not wanting to give her false hope. "I think it's unavoidable."

And it was very much unavoidable. I didn't tell her as I kissed her goodnight that my throat was hurting, and I'd cleverly hidden my sneezes inside of coughs throughout the day. When I laid my head down to sleep, the last thing I remembered was my feet starting to tingle, and I watched them earlier when I painted my nails a bright, glossy pink. When this whole thing was over, it would take twice as long.

October 12th, 2020

The next morning Ashleigh was already awake, as normal. I looked at her growth mark on the bathroom doorframe and saw that she'd gotten another six inches taller since yesterday morning.

I ran a hand across my stomach and felt a fine sheen of sweat. It was on my back too, as well as my forehead. I was so hot, my skin warm and tingly. And of course there were enough cases now to determine that these were the telltale signs that the growth was about to begin.

Ashleigh was in the living room watching television, so I decided to make my own mark. She kept the pen and the tape measure nearby, so it was easy to do. And just as I thought, I was two inches taller than normal.

She seemed relieved when I came into the living room, but she didn't notice that I was slightly bigger because she was growing too—it created the illusion that her own size increase wasn't so great.

"Morning," I said, fixing me a bowl of cereal and joining her on the sofa. Our feet were side-by-side, and I'll never forget how much bigger hers looked in that moment. Her toes were at least two inches past mine and although she was sitting down when I came into the room, I was sure that she was at least as tall as me now.

"You have it, don't you?" said Ashleigh, in a lot calmer voice than I would have guessed.

I thought for a moment to dodge, but finally I relented because how much longer could I possibly hide it?

"I do," I said. "How did you know?"

She reached down and rubbed a hand across my freshly painted toes. "Because you just did these yesterday, and already the natural nail is showing through on the sides."

"Ah."

"It'll be okay," she said, strangely the voice of reason.

"Let's measure our feet," I said, knowing she'd love the data. When she stood up, we were looking eye-to-eye. That could change throughout the day. So far, the virus didn't have a pattern. Women didn't grow a certain amount per day. It was sporadic, with test subjects shooting past one another on their way to the top.

It seemed as though our feet were growing disproportionately, at least by a little. Ashleigh's were fourteen inches long while mine were twelve. They still tingled, and we spent a lot of time that morning with our feet in one another's lap, massaging, working out the kinks and trying to make each other feel a little better.

By the time my ZOOM meeting rolled around at two o'clock, I was struggling with clothes. Up until now, we'd lived through the quarantine in only our pajamas. Now, I needed a blouse, a shirt, something that looked professional. It was all too tight. My breasts were squeezed in whatever I wore, and my biceps and forearms looked borderline masculine by the way they so tightly fit against the fabric. I chose to wear a large button-up shirt of Ashleigh's, knowing the camera would only capture my upper half. I sat in my desk chair in my undies.

If anything about this virus could be called beneficial, it was that the men of the world were doing most of the heavy lifting. It was the men who still reported to work, who took female shifts at the coffeehouses, who were on the front line to help society continue forward. Lucky ones like me and Ashleigh (if we could be called lucky) got to stay at home in our underwear on most days while the world sorted out this virus business.

When the ZOOM video chat loaded, it was Alexander who popped up first. He was still in the office building, editing stories as they came in from the work-from-home ladies. Next was Tabitha, the background behind her clearly that of her kitchen. So far she didn't seem symptomatic. A couple of other men loaded—Jack and Trevor—and finally a trio of girls—Angela, Beth, and Heidi.

All three of them were infected.

Angela was perhaps the most noticeable one. Her knees were blocking half the camera as she sat in front of her laptop. She was wearing a beach towel around her body, its fit rather snug, her breasts popping from the top. Her cycle was near its end, as she had to be around twelve feet tall.

Both Heidi and Beth were massive, although not as big as Angela. I placed these girls at around ten feet tall. Beth's size was a little harder to determine because she'd chosen to wear oversized clothes. The t-shirt (just as business appropriate as the beach towel) was probably a four-X. She let her long, auburn hair cascade down across her chest, hopeful to hide some of her mass. Heidi had always been rather miniscule, much like Ashleigh, but she had large breasts and a curvy body. Now, she was so plump because it was all magnified. She was wearing a bra and nothing more, although we couldn't see beneath the table. As I said before, there was no modesty with this virus.

"Ladies, I hope you're all well," said Jack, leading the meeting.

I won't bore the reader of my notes with what transpired, so I'll cut to the highlight. The most entertaining part came when the men asked Angela—the resident true giantess—why she was acting so glum when the rest of the girls seemed to be in good spirits.

"Why?" she responded. "Because I haven't been laid in a week! My husband won't touch me! Michael rocks a nine-inch cock! And he can't do a thing with it now. I'm sorry, I just . . . I just have to go." And then she stood up, the towel came open, and the entire office was treated to a twelve-foot woman's breasts and pussy before she exited out of frame.

Halfway through the meeting, Tabitha randomly announced that she thought she was infected. To showcase this, she reached under the table and pulled off her socks, then placed them next to her. Then, she lifted her feet onto the surface, extremely close to the camera.

"My feet are tingling," she said, a large thumb coming across to rub her sole. "I should've known it from the beginning. I'm so hot. I'm sweating all the time. My panties aren't fitting right."

"We know what you mean," said the other ladies. Each of them pulled their feet up and rested them on the table. I did it too. It was a quiet moment and we were there for each other in this tough time.

The rest of the meeting went rather well with the remaining women doing all they could to either hide their growing or to flaunt it. I could tell that Heidi loved how her breasts looked, and more than one of the men kept smiling as she adjusted, waiting for the tight bra to fire off like popcorn. I was waiting too, but no such luck.

"Hannah," said Trevor toward the end. "You're writing about all this, right?"

"I am."

"Good. Take care of yourself and each other."

"Okay, Ellen."

"What?"
"Nothing."

He stared a moment longer and finally said, "I look forward to your story."

After the meeting I took a shower and put on the baggiest pants and shirt I could find that wouldn't slip off me, but also allow me some growing room. But as I came into the bedroom, the shirt ripped at the edge, beneath the arm, and I knew I had grown in the short time since stepping out of the shower. I went over to the vanity in the corner, and no longer could I see my face. Now, the top of the mirror came to my throat, and as I stared at it, I could see tiny slivers of my flesh shining through, as the shirt was ripping, ever so subtly. I balled my hands into fists and noticed the same thing was happening at my sleeves. My clothes were quietly shredding all across my body.

Ashleigh was on the floor of the bedroom, her ass up in the air. I watched as her feet moved, toes clenching up so she could keep her balance on her knees.

"Your feet are massive," I said, bringing my own over and putting one on top of hers so they were flipped sole-to-sole. "It's kinda hot."

"Thanks," she said, still busy in her work.

"What are you doing?" I asked.

"Something I should've done from the beginning. I'm tracing my hands."

"Ah. Well I guess you should do mine too, huh?"

"Yeah, just let me grab another charcoal." She stood up, walked over to her box, and that's when I lost my breath.

"Shit, Ash."

"What?" she asked, but once we locked eyes, she knew.

My girlfriend was now looking down at me. It wasn't much, maybe just a couple of inches, but it was a radical difference from a day before when I could still kiss the top of her head. She put her hands up to her face, as if to hide her surprised tears, but I quickly pulled them away, then leaned in to kiss her. Already a tear had rolled down her cheek and I tasted the salt on my tongue. Still, she was shuttering when I wrapped my arms around her, and it was like hugging an entirely new person.

We spent the remainder of the evening on opposite ends of the sofa, comparing feet. Our sectional was extremely large, spanning the whole wall of our living room. I put my sole against hers and currently we were the same size. Both of us knew this wouldn't last, and it was anyone's guess who would pull ahead by tomorrow. Still, without comparing myself to her, it was a marked difference. The polish made it easy to see, the way the pink square continued to dwindle in the center of my toenails.

Sex was a little different—we both had a favorite toy. Mine was a pink vibrator that had a wand to stimulate my clit. Hers was a simple green dildo with deep ridges. And both of our toys were inadequate. Ashleigh, thus far, had grown the most, and her toy slipped into her comically, and the girl stood up only to have it slip out. The wand on my own sextoy got in the way of the actual shaft which now could fit further inside, if not for the part that stimulated my clit. We settled on the old-fashioned way, getting each other off with our fingers and tongues, but even that felt different. For better or worse, we were like two different women.

October 13th, 2020

The next morning we ate breakfast at the dining room table while listening to the news. More and more women were reaching what the top minds called the 'apex size' which meant they had stopped growing. And since the final height was a double-sized woman, not many women affected were below ten feet tall. This was creating a radical new way of life, for there didn't seem to be any strides made toward a cure or at the very least, a vaccine to prevent further outbreaks. The question now was what happened to the various women affected, now some sixty-million across the globe. Many were in quarantine and many more thought such isolation was silly. I was becoming one of them, but Ashleigh insisted that we stay in.

"What's the news say?" she said over cereal. "We flatten the curve of infection by taking ourselves out of society for a few weeks. I think if the two of us staying in this apartment lessens the infection rate, then we should by all means keep our growing asses here."

"I get that, sweetheart, I really do, but what about groceries?" I asked. "We're on our last gallon milk. There's half a loaf of bread and I don't have any bananas to make those smoothies you like."

"We'll deal with," she said. "Come look."

When she slid off the stool, I knew that she had changed—or I had. Now, she was looking like normal Ashleigh, a head shorter than me. Still, we were both bigger. She led me to the bedroom where she put her back against the doorframe and slashed a line above her head with the marker. The original mark was below her shoulders.

"I'm a fucking giant," she said, holding the tape measure up. "I'm one measly inch shy of eight feet!"

"Which means . . .," I said, my voice trailing off. I put my back to the adjacent doorframe and she measured.

". . . that you are eight and a half feet tall!"

"Jesus," I said, running fingers through my stringy blond hair.

Ashleigh was smiling. "Look at our latest hands and feet," she said.

We'd drawn three sets of each so far, the progression of growth in stark detail. Her feet had almost doubled in size while mine were getting close. Our current hands on top of the first drawings looked like we were holding children, and it was a little disconcerting to know that neither of us were at our final heights. But now, we were on the third day of growth, and for all the data known about Goliath, today was the day we would see the most marked changes.

"Has your feet tingled far more than normal today?"
I asked her around lunch as I read while she played some
video game that was far too noisy for my liking.

"Yeah," she said. "A lot more tingly."

I watched her after that. She was sitting cross-
legged on the floor, eyes up on the game, not paying any
attention to me. Ashleigh was in a pair of baggy pajama
pants and no shirt. The soles of her feet were facing me,
toes pulled in tight to keep her pose. And as I stared at the
beautiful wrinkles along her foot, I was captivated to see
them getting bigger before my eyes. Her toes were
stretching, her soles getting longer and wider. Ashleigh was
so enraptured by the game that she didn't even notice, only
stopping long enough to run a finger inside the tightening
waistband of her pants. It made me look at my own feet, to
note how my own soles were tingling. This brought up a
question I'd been wondering: Did all this time going
barefoot give me a foot fetish? It was entirely possible.

"Hey babe," I said, turning my attention back to her.
"You're growing again."

She paused the game and stood up, and now it was
more obvious than ever. The pajama pants ended above her
shins. There was a very noticeable camel toe forming at her
crotch. She brought her fingers down the sides of her pants
and pulled them out, the fabric ripping just enough to keep
them from being painful.

"How tall?" she asked, her voice sounding more
frustrated than fearful—and that was an improvement.

"You're pushing ten feet," I said, and when I stood
up, I was looking down at her. "Which makes me *over* ten
feet."

"Only one way to find out," she said. "Art project?"

"Art project."

On the way to the office, I noticed that my clothes were becoming ragged. My pants, panties, and shirt had holes in them, and as I moved, the tears became wider and longer. It was even audible, and as I stood there I the hallway, trailing behind Ashleigh, I could hear my pants rip right down the leg.

It was more fun for me to discover our growth through the foot and handprints. Where Ashleigh was more data driven and liked to see the readout of the doorframe, I preferred a more intrinsic approach. And when we dipped our feet in the yellow paint and stood on our pages, it was already apparent that we were much larger than yesterday. My feet were about eighteen inches long, probably disproportionate but still shapely and sexy. The square of pink looked dime-sized now. And just as I'd estimated in the living room, Ashleigh was two inches from being ten feet and I was ten feet and four inches high.

Getting through the apartment became increasingly more difficult. The doorframes were all seven feet tall, so we had to stoop to get through any of them. All of our cabinets felt off, as did using the toilet or shower. In the foyer we had to take a knee because we were constantly bumping the low-hanging chandelier. By the time we were winding down for bed, my back hurt because I had to hunch over so much to reach things meant for normal-sized people. Doorknobs, faucets, the refrigerator and stove. It was at this point that we decided to shed all clothes. None of our panties fit without discomfort, and the baggiest of pants were annoying when walking through the apartment. We closed the blinds (not that anyone could see on the seventy-fifth floor) and lived the remainder of quarantine in the nude.

We moved a cedar chest from the hall closet into the bedroom and placed it at the foot of our bed and then stacked pillows on top of it. Both of us were so long and lanky now that our calves hung over the edge of the bed. It was funny, to say the least. I looked for humor wherever I could find it, because deep down we were both scared—scared of the radical changes in our bodies and of how women were going to assimilate back into society. We couldn't go on forever inside this apartment.

"Look, the polish is all gone," said Ashleigh that night as we lay on our backs, legs extended to the air so we could compare feet. Currently mine were bigger, and would probably remain so from now on.

"They're all natural," I said.

"I kinda like it," said Ashleigh. "My feet are so big."

Do you know what that means?" I asked.

"What's that?" she asked, crinkling her toes.

"You only have a few more inches to go. And you'll be your final size. I still have around a foot left to grow."

"You'll probably get that tomorrow," she said, turning over and putting a hand across my breast. I stroked her hair as she leaned across me and popped my nipple into her mouth. Instantly it hardened, standing at attention. Sex was becoming an adventure. We were too large to have it the right way, but it was fun nonetheless. I went easy on her because Ashleigh was a squirter, and I didn't feel like

changing bedsheets because a ten-foot giantess gushed a
gallon of cum across our linens.

Before falling asleep to the news, I pulled up my
social media accounts and scrolled through what was
becoming of my friends. Everyone I knew was infected to
some degree. Some were just starting out, in denial,
refusing to leave their houses, while others were entering
their apex sizes and becoming massive giantesses. It was an
opportunity for girls to talk about clothing, diet, and
exercise. I wanted to peruse a little longer, but I found
myself drifting off, listening to the news.

October 14th, 2020

"I'm going to miss Halloween," said Ashleigh the
next morning. "I guess we'll still be here on the thirty-
first."

"We'll be out of food by the thirty-first," I said. It
was of little comfort, but it was true.

After breakfast we took turns on the recumbent bike
but it was too awkward to use now. Neither of us could fit
our feet into the stirrups, and our legs were so long that
even if we put our soles to the peddles, it was hard to keep
enough momentum to keep them going. But after my
twenty-minute attempted workout, I stood up, and my head
brushed the ceiling. I was there. I was at my final height,
which was two inches short of twelve feet.

We tried yoga again since the bike wasn't going to
service us any longer. Now, it was a little more awkward
because we certainly couldn't raise our hands. I thought it
was quite odd and an interesting that the last time we did

this we were much smaller. Both of us felt like goddesses now.

"Ash, come here," I said. She was in the bedroom, playing a handheld gaming system while listening to some zombie show on Netflix.

She entered the office, ducking down to clear the doorway. When her eyes fell upon me, she giggled. "Damn girl, you got some nice tits!"

"That's all you can say?" I asked, laughing and grabbing them, fingers tweaking my own nipples.

"I guess this is our new size," she said. "You're eleven feet and ten inches and I'm ten feet and six inches. What a fucking world we live in."

"You're being dramatic," I said, only I felt the same way. I was just better at not verbalizing it.

"Maybe. I've been looking up a few sites that have popped up since Goliath. Both *Old Navy* and *Forever 21* have started selling 'Apex' clothing for women sized ten to twelve feet tall. Some of it's really cute."

"You'll have to show me later," I said, and just like that we both conceded the point that this was our new normal. That we would forever be stuck at double our former sizes.

We spent that evening feeling better than ever. All of the lingering symptoms flitted away. There were no sore throats, no headaches, no fever or sweating. All that remained was drastically enlarged women. Was this so bad? I wondered. Perhaps if it had been just me and Ashleigh. But the news showed so many women across the globe, many who were going back to work, filling the roles they'd left during the quarantine. It was only a matter of time before my paper would ask me to return. Might as well make the best of it, I decided.

Later, we did more feet and hand comparisons. Holding our palms up was the same as it had been when we were normal-sized. My scale was the same in relation to hers. But it was an amazing thought to know our feet had literally doubled in size. My toes were so long, so thick. When we finished the art project, we had rainbow butterflies made up of our feet. My final one was twenty inches long and hers was eighteen inches. We hung them on the hallway wall, and Ashleigh assured me that once life resumed as normal, we'd go to the craft store and have them framed.

October 15th, 2020

This morning I woke up to Ashleigh pulling at my shoulders. When I saw her, my first response was that something was wrong, that she'd forgotten to take the foil off her Hot Pocket and the apartment was on fire, or that we had a burglar. It wouldn't be the first time something like that happened in our building, but it would be the first time a would-be robber would have the shit beaten out of him by two scared and angry giantesses. But no, as my eyes adjusted I could tell she was happy—overjoyed and ecstatic.

"What is it?" I asked.

"Come see, come see!" She ran out of the bedroom, almost banging her head on the doorframe.

I followed with far less enthusiasm, rubbing the sleep from my eyes. The television was on, a newscaster who was clearly a giantess by the way her clothes were ill-fitted across her shoulders, was interviewing a doctor wearing a mask. Across the bottom read: BREAKING NEWS IN MOLLY HAMILTON CASE. I was too sleepy to make sense of that name but it finally did come to me.

"Wasn't she the first lady to grow?"

"Yeah!" said Ashleigh, clapping her hands. "And guess what? She's shrinking!"

"What?"

"Yeah! They said she was four inches shorter last night and they think it's going to keep happening."

"That's . . . great!" I said. "It's just like the flu. We're 'getting over' it."

"Seems that way," said Ashleigh.

Suzanne Martel came on the screen, and for the first time since quarantine, she was back in the studio. Now, she was apex sized, and wearing a very revealing dress that had been made just for her. She was barefoot, as the camera did a slow, but steady sweep of her whole body. Now that the virus was known to go away, she wasn't staying inside any longer.

"You heard it here first, friends," she said. "The uncertainty we've had these last few months will be going away. I will be back to my regular six-foot status. Chuck, back to you."

We sat there in silence, watching the news unfold. There'd been so many negative stories lately, and for once this one felt like a win. I sat opposite her again on the sectional, still long enough to accommodate two giantesses. Our soles touched, and it made me a little sad to think that we would be losing this size. The more I dwelled on it, the more I'd come to own what my life had become, the more at ease it put me. And now, as strange as it sounded, I was a little dejected that my size would soon be stripped away.

"You alright?" she asked, sensing my silence as being introspective.

"Yeah. I just . . . I think I'm going to miss being a giantess."

"Oh. I get that." And then she swung her leg around and straddled me. She leaned in and gave me a kiss. That's when we heard the groan beneath us, the weight of two giant women bearing down on a flanking section of the furniture. All four legs beneath us snapped and we yelped as the whole thing collapsed.

"At least we won't be dangerous!" I said.

She leaned in again, atop the ruin of our sectional and said, "that's a pity," and then she kissed me again.

March 31st, 2021

The story was a success but I wasn't writing about anything the world didn't already know. We were infected, we grew, and in a month, we started to shrink back down to normal. It took a lot longer to get small than it did to get big. But at the end of a three-week span, we were once more our correct height. Stores reopened, remote work stopped, as did distant learning for the schools. Supply chains balanced out and probably the best part of all, we could go see people again.

We had a party at the apartment months after the growth had reversed. Ashleigh and I shared work friends and we invited all of the ladies we knew. This was a global event that linked the women together in solidarity. The men wouldn't understand. So that night, I sat in our living room, entertaining almost fifteen women who'd been infected.

"How has work been for you guys?" I asked the room.

Angela was the first to speak up, carefully nursing her drink. "They're nicer to me, which is good. I was a real bitch while I was big."

"Me too," said Tabitha. "It's been weird to work around people who have seen you completely naked."

Ashleigh and I looked at each other. "That hasn't been our experience."

"Really?" asked Heidi. "I loved my giant body but I dunno . . ."

"Let's talk about a side effect," I said. "Be honest, ladies. Do you still have the tingly feeling every now and then? Isn't barefoot so much better?"

They all murmured agreements.

"And while we're being honest," said Ashleigh. She lifted her shirt off and tossed it into the floor. The room of ladies looked at her wordlessly. "Doesn't it feel better without clothes?"

For a moment, there was silence. And then, one by one, the girls started to strip out of their clothes. Angela, Heidi, Tabitha, all women with fantastic bodies shed their garments and made a giant pile in the middle of the room.

And finally, even I stood up and joined them, feeling somewhat freer now that the virus had run its course. But it certainly left us with crippled inhibitions. I pulled my shirt off and danced out of my jeans. Now, I was sitting amongst a crowd of naked, beautiful women.

I smiled. "*Now* it's a party."

Message Board Giantess

He hated these trips to the east coast but he loved his mother, so he didn't have much choice. After his dad passed away, Nick flew out to Pennsylvania quite a bit, and it was much different than his own city of Seattle. Mainly, his mom lived in a little burg right outside of Philadelphia, and it was lacking of any sort of entertainment. He was used to being able to go places, get a good cup of coffee and good food, but not here. In the little town of Howster, he was struggling to have a good time.

It was his mom's birthday, and although she had many colleagues from work who showed up to throw her a party, she didn't have many people in the way of family. Nick wasn't even the closest—mom had two sisters, but both were older and didn't travel very well. He hated the idea that she'd spend the holidays alone. And since Nick didn't have a significant other, certainly no kids, he volunteered to spend those milestones with her. Ever since they lost his dad, his mom hadn't spent a Thanksgiving, Christmas, New Year's, or birthday alone. Nick had made sure of that.

She was early to bed each night, and the one saving grace of visiting was the quiet time he got after dark to peruse his favorite websites. Mainly he surfed the giantess community—a string of sites dedicated to the adoration of giant and growing women. Nick had a kink, a rather *odd* kink, but one that drove him crazy just the same. There were many like him out there, although he'd never met one in person. He always assumed the desire was latent, that many people probably had it inside them, but only a few were blessed (or cursed) enough to have it wake up. Nick was glad that it did, because the daydreams that occurred were some of the best in the world.

But the night before he left to go back home, he noticed a new site had popped up within the community. It was called Big Girls/Little Guys Dating. He was thrown by the name, but could it be exactly how it sounded? Nick thought he'd check it out, and just as he guessed, it was a dating site for those who were interested in the giantess fetish. Not surprising was the fact that nearly eighty percent of the users were male. Still, twenty percent was a good fraction of girls who were into the fantasy. He had always put that number closer to zero.

Most of the women on the site were spread out across the globe. A large cluster of them was Asiatic, around Japan. Several of them were surely not his type, and a few didn't even have a full profile, or had a cat or some kind of anime character as a profile photo. But he did see one girl that he thought was rather cute.

Her profile read:

Shelley Gentry – 25 years old, loves being the big one. Looking for a man who is like-minded and would love to have a little size discussion. Feel free to hit me up!

She was in Massachusetts, not terribly far from where he was currently sitting, but a country away from where he'd be tomorrow. Still, he found her rather interesting, especially when she listed her favorite size-themed movies. She was very much like him, on more than just the fetish level. So, he got brave, opened his UniChat program and put in her ID. And then, he sent a message. Just a simple hello and that he'd seen her on the dating site.

Within thirty seconds, she'd sent one back:

Hello, Nick from Seattle!

Hey. So you're really a girl?

She went quiet after that, and he was worried that he'd chased her off. But a photo quickly filled his phone. It matched the profile above—a gorgeous red-haired girl with freckles, only the latest picture showed her with a very stern expression, as if she were offended that he would even ask the question.

Okay, so you're a girl.

Mmmhmm. Where you from, cutie? I'm guessing you're a cutie, right?

He ran a hand through his hair, took a picture he thought wasn't terrible, added a filter, and then sent it to her.

Not bad at all. So where are you from? she asked again.

Seattle, but currently in Pennsylvania.

Not too far. I should stomp my way there now.

Her words made his heart race. *Oh yeah? Well c'mon.*

Lucky for you, I drank my last growing potion earlier and I've already shrunk back down.

Oh, I like you, he said.

Yeah? You seem alright yourself. Tell me more.

And he went on to tell her much, much more. They chatted well into the night, talking about everything from their personal lives. She worked at a game store in a strip mall. She had two brothers and one sister. Her favorite food was spaghetti and she went to community college for fashion design. But the real 'meat' of their conversation was when it turned to giantess things, and they discovered just how much they had in common.

They didn't like the same things within the fetish, that would've been redundant and boring. Instead, their interests complimented one another. He fantasized about being shrunken down to a foot tall. She fantasized about doing just that. Nick was short for a guy, standing at five-feet even, and one of his biggest fantasies was to have sex with a mini-giantess—someone seven or eight feet tall. She told him if she were close, she would make that happen. It was a nice way to phrase the roleplay, but little did he know, she could make it all come true.

Nick fell asleep talking to Shelley, and she fell asleep talking to him. They both realized the other was exactly what they'd been searching for, and both hoped, although neither said it, that they would one day meet. It was a slim possibility, but Nick took that idea back to Seattle with him. At the very least, he had met a new friend who loved the same thing as he did.

He fantasized about such a meeting. What would it be like? He'd dated plenty of girls but had never had the courage to bring up his rather unique kink. While it was normal for him, it might be off-putting to most women. Shelley was like a unicorn and he was thankful that he finally had someone to bounce ideas from. Nick liked to write stories, and he wasn't such a bad artist, either. He created lots of giantess art, and for the first time in his life, he had someone to show. And Shelley loved his creations.

She wasn't such a bad artist herself, although her stuff dabbled in animation. He'd been a fan of those digital cartoons for years, the ones where people used three-dimensional people and then made them grow and shrink.

Shelley was a master at such things, and he loved to see her new posts on the giantess boards.

As much as he wanted a meeting during his stay at his mom's house, it simply wasn't in the cards. He had to return to work, had a plane to catch, and although Massachusetts was close to Pennsylvania, relatively speaking, it was an impossible trip, even if they both met halfway. So, the following day, Nick boarded a plane and returned to Seattle, longing to talk to his new giantess friend. When the plane landed, it was almost a punch to his gut, for he felt the distance now with every fiber of his being. It was insurmountable, and he knew that he would never see this girl, not in person, at least. But thankfully they were in the golden age of technology, and if he couldn't be standing before her, he could at least have her on a screen.

And he was able to get screen time quite often.

She made his life much better. Neither of them had many friends, so they turned to each other quite frequently for support and comfort. Message board chats led to Facebook friends. And then on to Snapchat, Twitter, and Instagram. Finally, the most coveted of all communications, they exchanged numbers, left the kiddie stuff in the dust and began texting like adults. They rarely went more than an hour without sending something to the other, even if it was a simple meme or joke.

Their relationship became a little more substantial after just a month. She started sending him nudes—well, not full-nude—just boob shots. He was such a boob man, and Shelley didn't disappoint. She was rocking some of the largest breasts he'd ever seen. Whenever she sent something nice to his phone, it was never a full-body shot, nor did she show her face in the same pics as her breasts.

He wondered if it was a trust thing or if she were simply self-conscious. He didn't mind girls with a little extra meat on their bones, but he felt awkward saying such a thing.

"Do you think you'd actually like me if you met me?" she asked late one night on the phone. He loved talking to her more than texting, as her voice was lovely.

"That's a silly question," he said. "Of course I would."

"Don't be so sure, little man," she said. "Sometimes the fantasy is better than reality. I've often wondered what it would be like to watch a man shrink before my eyes. But if I actually had that in front of me, would it be as sexy as my mind makes it out to be?"

"It would be sexy to me," he said. "If I were the man shrinking."

"Oh really now?" she said, her voice sliding into a playful purr.

"Most definitely, my goddess."

"I love it when you call me that."

"Then I'll call you that forevermore."

"I like the sound of that," she said.

***

Not much changed in their relationship over the next few weeks. They roleplayed a little, mostly exchanging texts because he loved to save them and read them again later. But anytime he tried to get her to do something on camera, she shied away, as if she were hiding something. They'd grown so close that he couldn't understand her reluctance, but still he wasn't ready to broach the subject. And then, almost six months to the day after they'd started talking, he learned that he wouldn't have to bring it up at all.

He was coming out of work—she knew his schedule quite well and always sent him a text as he was walking through the door. When he was fastening the seatbelt in his car, he looked at the message and found it was only a picture. It took a moment to understand what he was seeing, not because it was something so farfetched, but because it was something incredibly ordinary. He was looking at Brewster's Coffee Shop, his favorite littles spot, only half a mile from his house.

I don't understand, he said, replying back. *That's my favorite place.*

I know.

Why are you sending me this? He was still confused.

After a few seconds she sent another photo, of the same coffee shop, only this time, she was in the pic, smiling greatly.

No way . . .

I'm a mile from you right now.

How? Why? OMG!!

You headed home? I have to stop and get gas for my rental car and then I'll come over. How's that sound?

Um, sounds amazing. You know how to find my place?

Nope, but my map app does. See you soon.

***

His hands were shaking as he drove home, arriving much faster than normal because he wanted to get there first. His house was a bit of a mess, and he struggled trying to get it picked up before she pulled into his driveway. Nick loaded the dishwasher, picked up an assortment of take-out containers from the living room, hid the dirty clothes in the hamper, and finally picked up his video game pile from the floor. He was upstairs, changing and running a comb through his wild hair when there was a loud, powerful knock on the door. Of course she wouldn't be dainty, he thought. Her knock could probably break down the door.

He came back downstairs, doing his best to steady his nerves. Nick swallowed the lump in his throat and quickly jerked the door open, not sure what he would say when he saw her. A tiny part of him wondered if she were right—if there would be something about her, some strange personality quirk, that made him not like her. But as the door opened and a dress swelled across his field of vision, such thoughts went out the window. Before him stood the girl he'd flirted with on the internet for half a year. The girl who'd sent him pictures of her breasts. The girl who'd roleplayed with him and said she wanted to use him as her own personal sextoy. It was Shelley, the goddess herself.

And she was standing at around eight feet tall.

"Shelley, my god. You're . . . you're really . . . um."

"Big?" she said, slightly bending her knees so she could look him in the eyes.

"Yeah," he said. "I'm sorry. Um, you just caught me off-guard. Come on in." He backed up so she could enter, which wasn't easy for someone of her size. Shelley had large breasts, even relative to her size. When she entered through the doorway, she had to turn sideways, and her breasts and voluminous ass got caught on the frame. It was rather comical, but right now he was throbbing so hard in his pants that he barely registered anything besides arousal.

She was dragging an overnight bag behind her, which was the size of a small refrigerator. The clothes that she wore had to be special order, for he'd never seen garments so large. Just her shoes alone—dainty flats that were not dainty in size—had to be around fourteen inches long. She rolled her suitcase to the corner by the door and looked around his living room. She put a hand to her hip and said, "It's smaller than I imagined."

"I guess it's all small to you," said Nick. "Have a seat. Can I get you a drink?"

"That sounds lovely, dear." She assessed his furniture and then sat on his leather sofa. That was his favorite spot, and as he moved over to the kitchen to grab a bottle of wine and two glasses, he thought that he couldn't wait to be sitting there next to her.

As he watched her from behind the island, he couldn't help but be overcome with arousal. She was literally his fantasy—although he liked the size difference to be a little more pronounced. Shelley was the closest thing he'd ever seen to an actual giantess. But even if she were normal-sized, she had one of the best bodies he'd ever seen. The two biggest factors for him were ass and tits— and she had enormous ones all around.

"Care to tell me how you're sitting in my living room right now?" he asked, returning with the wine glasses. When she took hers, it looked comically small in her hand, and it would be gone in just a swallow. However, she took a micro-sip and patted the seat next to her for him to sit down. Now, he was looking up at her, and felt every inch of her size.

"I had frequent flyer miles left over from my last job and they were going to expire. I didn't know if this was a good idea or not, Nick. A little voice in my head kept telling to abort. But I stepped on that voice. And now here I am." She drained her wine, swirled it in her mouth and said, "That's good. More please?"

He did as the goddess asked, resting the bottle on the coffee table next to them. She'd pushed the table out a little while he was in the kitchen to accommodate her legs. Nick couldn't pull his eyes from them, and he wanted very much to dive under her dress. He'd talked about doing that very thing on so many occasions, but now with the giantess in front of him, he couldn't seem to bring himself to say it.

"So," he began, not sure of how to proceed. "You're an actual giantess."

"I guess an amazon would be closer to the truth," she said. "You're into giantess stuff, you should know your sizes."

He laughed. "Okay, you got me there. But you're way bigger than a normal person. You know that, right?"

She put a finger up to her cheek in mocking thought. "You know, now that you mention it. I did have a little trouble getting through your doorway."

"Very funny."

She laughed and put a hand on his leg, to which the throbbing in his pants intensified. "I know I'm big. I've always been a little taller than most. And that's what brought me to the giantess community in the first place. And it's what propelled my research."

"Research?"

"Yeah, I've been working on a size formula. And guess what? It works."

"No way," he said, draining his own wine. "Not possible."

"It is possible," she said. "I'm normally just seven feet tall."

"You're crazy, but I love it," he said, not believing a word of what she told him. She smiled gently and leaned in to kiss him. Her lips were large, almost swallowing his own. He leaned back into the kiss and pulled on her hair, wrapping the strands around his fingers.

"I'm glad your shyness went away," she said, leaning back. She fixed him with those large, green eyes that he'd fallen in love with months ago thought pictures.

"It didn't take long once you showed up."

After that, an awkward silence hung in the room, and finally she looked up the stairway behind them and said, "That the way to your bedroom?" He would have thought it was an innocent question if not for the way she was grinning at him.

His face turned red and he said, "Yeah. Want the tour?"

She stood up, her giant breasts nearly blocking the view of her face from where he sat, and said, "I most definitely do." Shelley returned to her suitcase and pulled out a thin case along the side. Without saying a word, she stood and waited, then held out a hand, instructing him to lead on.

He took her upstairs to the bedroom, the first door on the left. Nick slept in a queen-sized bed which was perfect for him, but not so much for two people. And certainly not enough if one of them happened to be an amazon. He sat on the edge of the bed and looked up at her as she slowly strolled into the room. She placed the case on the bed next to him and then dropped to her knees. Now, he could see down the top of her dress, could almost see a nipple if only she'd stretch back a little. But his eyes quickly averted to hers as she fixed him with a seductive stare, and then her hands were on his thighs.

Her long fingers quickly unbuckled his belt, and when she slid his pants down, he worried his dick wouldn't measure up to what she needed. Nick was somewhat endowed, especially for such a small guy, and when she pulled back his shirt to see his cock flop against his stomach, she made a little moan. As her hand wrapped around it, he certainly felt her size—and his own lack of it.

"Gonna tear me up with this?" she asked, then descended on it without waiting for a response, her mouth making slurping sounds. It had been so long since he'd had a proper blowjob, and this one was shaping up to be a good one. Her jaws were so powerful, the force of her sucking incredible. She had great technique—sucking, swirling her tongue around his head, parting her lips and dragging them across his shaft. And even when she went back to stroking, it was the perfect rhythm, although he was small enough to slip out of her fingers. The veins in his dick throbbed, and just when he was afraid he would blow his load, she let go, sucking off the head with a pop. "Not so fast, little man."

She sat back on her haunches and lifted the dress over her head, a small silver pendant her only piece of clothing now. He barely noticed the dangling necklace, so large and all-encompassing her breasts were. She had gorgeous, dark nipples, the areolas like discs. Shelley braced herself on the bed next to him and leaned up so he could pop a nipple into his mouth. She made a tiny cry and he could feel her body relax, so he used both hands to massage her mounds while taking turns between nipples. At the end, they were hard as nails, and he couldn't help but tweak them.

Shelley pushed him up, and he crawled backwards to the head of the bed. Then, she walked up on her knees, descending her pussy down right on top of his waiting cock. Although she was big, it was still a nice fit, and a warm shiver ran through her body once her pussy lips were touching the base of his cock. She started to ride, slowly, and the bed creaked in protest. Her long hair was cascading across his breasts.

"Do you wanna have some *real* fun?" she asked him.

"Is this not real fun?" he asked, confused.

"No, darling. I come bearing gifts." And then, she dragged the case up next to her and flipped back the lid.

Inside rolled several tiny vials, each containing a different color of liquid. Seeing them was enough to get his juices flowing. She'd roleplayed this very scenario with him so many times, and he loved the idea of doing it in person. Shelley picked one that contained a pale green solution, uncapped it, and then drank it down. She made a little shiver, as if the stuff had a bad aftertaste.

"It always packs a punch," she said. "Now where were we?" She leaned in, put her hands on his shoulders and picked up the pace, riding him slow but hard.

And that's when he noticed.

Not only had her strength increased—her hands were becoming painful on his shoulders—but her breasts had seemed to double in size. Her nipples were elongating with each bounce. And then, it was unmistakable that her body was spreading out, that Shelley was growing. The bed was bowing horribly now, and with each thrust of her hips the frame seemed closer and closer to death. His dick was slipping out now, not meant to occupy the pussy of a woman who was fast approaching twelve feet tall. But it didn't matter. She'd leaned in low, was dragging her clit across his body, and then he felt her explode with warm juices. Shelley's whole body shuddered.

"Holy fuck!" said Nick when she moved to the side. "You. . . you . . . grew!"

"I told you it was my research, silly." She held up a hand and turned it over while staring at it. Nick could tell this wasn't 'old hat' to her, and that growing was possibly a new venture for her.

"Is it permanent?" he asked.

"If I want it to be," she said. "But otherwise it'll wear off by morning."

She descended on his dick again, and this time it was like a monster coming at him, for all he could see was hair and lips. Shelley sucked him, but he could tell she was holding back because at her current size, she would probably pull his dick right off. It didn't take her long to get the job done—after all, this was all his fantasy.

They talked about her potions for a long while after that, and Nick couldn't understand the science behind it. Still, he was more turned on than he'd ever been in his life. But eventually they moved out of the bedroom and downstairs. He cooked her dinner—pasta and garlic bread—and made sure to fix a family-sized portion because she would most likely need to eat double. It was amazing to see her prancing around in his house, her head brushing the ceiling. He'd made sure to pull all the blinds and curtains before she came downstairs.

They took their plates back up to the bedroom became it was the most comfortable spot where she could sit. The sofa was too narrow to accommodate her now massive, bulbous ass. When she sat on the bed, it seemed to spread out in all directions. Likewise, her breasts seemed to have undergone the same disproportionate growth, and she comically rested her plate on top of them while she ate.

"So what do the rest of those do?" Nick asked a little while later after they'd finished up. He was pointing to the case where sat a collection of vials—red, green, blue, and a few even clear.

"Different things. I want you to try one when you're ready."

"Oh? Which one?" he said, pulling the case up to his lap.

"The red one."

He pulled it out and uncapped it, giving it a tiny sniff. "It's safe?"

"Of course."

"What will it do to me?"

She just grinned. "I don't want to ruin the surprise. But you'll be quite happy."

That was all the reason he needed. He turned it up, then drained the whole thing and replaced the empty vial in the case.

Quickly she cleared the plates and took the case away, moving them all to the side of the bed. "Take your clothes off now, sweetie," she said. "It'll be easier that way."

He stood up to undress and as he was pulling his legs through his pants, he felt a sudden wave of dizziness. "Woah," he said.

"It'll pass," she assured, then took his dick in her mouth again and started to suck while he stood next to the bed. Shelley had flopped over on her breasts and was lying across the mattress, legs and feet hanging down on the other side.

Nick's body was changing. He could see the world spreading out, growing larger. The ceiling shot up, the walls moved away, and Shelley's lips slowly became thicker and fuller. When he was roughly half his size, she grabbed him around the thighs in her massive hands and lifted him up. He braced himself across the top of her head. It was an odd sensation to feel her hair expanding beneath his forearms.

When she was lying back on the bed, his feet were standing atop her breasts, and as he continued to dwindle, it was slightly scary by how large she'd become. Her mouth was so big, so wet. And when she couldn't fit him inside it anymore, he backed up, and now her face was all he could see. He didn't know how small he'd gotten. Perhaps only a foot tall, but as she flicked his stomach and sent him rolling down the mound of her breasts, he realized he was perfect.

He landed just between her legs, and now he was staring right into her giant, wet pussy. They were both professionals when it came to this fantasy, so there was no dawdling, no wondering what the other person wanted. Nick charged forward, parting her lips. He was big enough to be a tight fit, and as her back arched off the bed, his feet left the mattress. When she settled down, he continued, pushing himself right into her.

It was very much how he imagined it in his fantasy. She was wet, warm, sticky—all of those great things he'd hoped it would be. And most importantly, she was just tight enough for him to get enough traction to pull himself deeper. With each movement, she tightened, as if to tell Nick to slow down. But when he could go no further, he rolled back around, feeling as though he were being hugged in her muscles.

He wasn't running out of air as he thought he would be, but that didn't mean she wouldn't flood him with juices. Still, he kicked his legs and shoved his arms into her flesh, and each time she grew warmer and wetter. This was a ride he'd dreamed about for years, and she didn't let him down when she came—completely gushing him out where he landed between her quivering thighs.

After that, she let him rest, and then he went right back in. He played inside until his strength left him completely, but luckily he was able to jerk off on the last round, his cum almost nonexistent inside the chasm of his goddess. Nick fell asleep on her ass cheek that night, and he didn't even feel her move him when she got up and checked out his backyard. Things would be different tomorrow . . . yet again.

***

When he woke up the next morning, he could feel his body was changed. His legs were hanging off the edge of the bed and he had the momentary idea that he'd grown much bigger, as she had been when she couldn't sleep comfortably on the mattress. But no, he'd only been near the edge when he'd grown back. And when he sat up and took in his surroundings, it was a small relief that the formula was reversible. Nick was back to his normal five feet, but Shelley was nowhere to be found. Would she be seven feet tall now? Shorter? He didn't know. He'd only seen her giant-sized and the thought of her being anything less made him a little sad.

He was just about to get out of bed when the ground shook. He stopped in his tracks. It shook again and the plates from the nightstand fell into the floor and shattered. Nick didn't notice at all, for he'd already fled down the steps, following the ground-shaking until he ripped open the back door and stepped into the yard, only to be confronted by a giant foot directly in front of him. He followed it up, and there standing in his yard, ruining his lawn, was Shelley, only she was much, much larger.

They were roughly scaled the same as yesterday, in relation to each other, but oh, how the roles had been changed. She was every inch a giantess now. No amazon, no mini, just simply giantess.

Or goddess.

"Morning," she said. "I may have given myself the wrong dosage."

"You think?" he said, but he was smiling.

"I forgot that I needed to shrink back first. My twelve-foot metabolism is all crazy. So this is the result. You don't mind, do you?"

"Definitely not," he said, stroking his dick.

"Then get in here," she said, reaching down and grabbing him. She took a knee—which sent a shockwave through the neighborhood, and then he was being lifted, headfirst, into her waiting pussy.

It was much the same as before, only now he was fighting gravity because she was upright. Still, the more he pushed forward and the more she shoved, the tighter she became, and he didn't fear being dropped. This time, it was much easier to get her off, as she was slightly tighter than before and his arms and legs were more effective. When she did cum, he felt himself slipping, and he let out a tiny scream, but just as she opened up and he fell, her hand was beneath him to catch him. She lifted his tiny body into the air and looked him over, then licked him clean.

Finally, she set him back on the ground. He couldn't even see her face because her breasts were so large and were blocking her whole head, but he could hear her voice.

"Like it?" she said.

"Definitely. You've still got more potions."

"That I do," she said. "Care if I stay the week?"

He smiled. "Yes ma'am. But you gotta sit down. The neighbors are gonna say something!"

The Dream Nurse

Chuck had been in car crashes before, but nothing like this one. He'd wrecked his dirt bike when he was seventeen and had twenty-eight stitches from his ankle to his hip. He'd flipped his Geo Metro turning off the freeway after catching ice when he was twenty-two. That netted him a broken collarbone. And then there was the time he was with his ex-girlfriend, travelling down the I-77 when a semi failed to brake at the intersection and it plowed right into them. The entire front of the little Cavalier was mangled, but they'd escaped the worst of it. But now, he had a new accident under his belt, and he wasn't sure he'd be as lucky to come away unscathed.

The last thing he remembered was pulling up to the intersection on Howard Street, then turning left. Then, his car stalled—it had a transmission problem that he'd neglected to fix for some time now, but this was a busy spot, on Labor Day weekend, and it was dangerous to idle in such a place. He was about to step out of the car, to look under the hood, to remedy it with whatever was in his limited skillset. Had he not dawdled a little longer inside the car, he wouldn't have been able to have any of these thoughts. His whole body would've been creamed against the grill of a truck. But said truck hit his door, slamming hard with so much force that it was like the world was ending inside.

Glass shattered, wheels screeched, someone screamed—most likely him. And then the whole car was flipping fast, end over end. It was raining popcorn—that was his last lucid thought because he'd had an opened bag of it in his glove compartment. His neck was jerking awkwardly, but he'd been wearing his seatbelt which, after everything was over, may or may not have been a blessing. When the car came to rest, still sliding across the pavement, he barely heard the voices approaching. He was upside down, and his eyes were stinging. His last thought before blacking out was that it was because blood was running into them.

The next few moments, or days, or weeks for all he knew was a mixture of flashing lights, sounds, voices, and smells. His body wasn't in pain, and that worried him. Shouldn't he have felt like a flayed fish by now? He kept drifting in and out of consciousness, most likely because of the drugs. Was he in a coma? He wasn't sure. One thing he did know was that when bouts of lucidity hit him, he was far more aware than he would've guessed.

Sometime after the accident, he remembered hearing voices—two lovely females that probably would've given him a hard-on should that part of his brain still function. But they sounded disembodied, very large, as if they were either massive or just high up. The way his mind was wired, and because of the nature of his business, it made him consider the former.

"Do you know who this is?" asked the first voice, Nurse One as he thought of her to keep the people on the other side of his eyelids straight.

"Gosh, he looks so familiar," said Nurse Two.

"That's Chuck Atwell," said Nurse One.

"No way!" Nurse Two exclaimed. "The guy who was in Shrinking Tom and The Giantess in the Cupboard?"

"Yes! Oh, geez, he's kinda hot, isn't he?"

"More than kinda hot."

If Chuck could smile in his state, he would.

He was one of the most well-known actors working in the size business. That's what the industry called anyone who dabbled in the fine art of making women look gigantic and men look absolutely miniscule. It was a sexual fetish that was climbing the ranks. Even *Playboy* did a story on it a few months back, citing that it was the fastest growing kink in the United States. Chuck had made a fine living doing it, and was probably one of the wealthiest people in the community. For two random nurses to recognize him was a testament to his success and influence.

"Is he going to make it?" asked Nurse Two.

"I think so. But he's going to be out for a while."

"Do you think . . ." The nurse's voice trailed off, but then she finished, in a whisper. "Do you think he'd be a candidate? You know, for the machine?"

"I'm going to ask," said Nurse One. "I mean, c'mon. It's Chuck fucking Atwell. He can heal and I can see what it's like to be in one of his movies."

"You're so bad," said the other nurse. "But I like it."

After that, the voices melded into his brain, replaced by a dull thump. He was in so much pain, but it came and went, most likely due to whenever they decided to pump him full of meds. Were they monitoring his brain? He wondered why he was able to feel so much, and to know so much that was happening around him. A part of Chuck thought that maybe he was dead, and that this was some sort of purgatory he was having to live through before being sorted to his soul's final resting place.

But then, things changed dramatically.

One day (or perhaps night for the unconscious state was an unending ordeal) he opened his eyes. The room around him was lit with small, votive candles that smelled of honey and lavender. There was thick, plush carpet on the floor, and the ceiling was tiled, arranged with curly patterns. He sat up and looked down. Chuck was wearing only blue jeans and nothing else. No shoes, no shirt, no service. These weren't even a pair of pants that he recognized. His chest was a little sweaty, but it didn't look to be in any shape like he'd expected. He drew in a deep breath, and he felt fine.

And at that point he figured he was surely dead. There was no other explanation for why he should be feeling so . . . *alive*. The room around him must have been some sort of purgatory, what with its bare walls and dark corners. He couldn't even see how far it went, his eyes only focusing a few feet beyond the small table holding the votive lights.

"Hello, Chuck," a voice purred to his left. He immediately recognized it to belong to Nurse One.

He turned to her and was able to put a face with the voice, and was not disappointed in the least. She was a rather short woman with long, curly blond hair. She was dressed in purple scrubs with matching shoes. As she approached, it was almost as if she were floating, so quick and effortless that she traversed the room. When she was standing before him, her bright blue eyes seemed to bore into his soul. Was she an angel? No creature of hell could be this beautiful.

"I'm sure you're very confused right now," she said. "My name is Ellie. And no, you're not dead."

"Oh thank God," he said, visibly relieved.

"Don't celebrate too much, because you're not exactly alive either. Not without the help of a special machine."

"I don't understand," he said.

"Right now, you are asleep. You are in a critical care unit in a very experimental hospital. You've suffered numerous broken bones—more than I care to name, actually. But the crux of your problem is the brain. You have some severe swelling to go along with a series of cranial fractures. You rolled across glass when the car flipped and those things have caused quite a bit of damage."

Just hearing it made him sick. "Am I going to be alright?"

"You might. But it'll take time. And thanks to the latest advances in medically-induced coma practices, you've been hooked up to the Dream Machine. I know, it sounds silly, but that's what it is."

"Care to explain?"

"Certainly. While you're under, we're able to turn your brainwaves into something tangible. In here, you can pretty much do whatever you want. This is the Matrix, Chuck. Or at least the closest thing we've got to it."

"So you're not real?" he asked, a little dejected.

She looked offended. "I'm hurt, good sir. I'm very much real. I can link up to you through the machine. Currently I'm lying on a cot just next to you. And I'm glad I did it." This last bit she said in a seductive voice, carefully biting her bottom lip.

"You are?"

"Yes. I'm sure you hear this all the time, but . . . I'm your biggest fan."

"Really?" He couldn't believe it at all.

"Oh yes. And if you'd like, we could . . . discuss our mutual fantasy. Seems to me that all you have right now, is time."

"I think I would like that very much," he said, still perplexed by the concept of a 'Dream Machine.' Things felt normal here. As he moved, he felt the weight of his body, the slight breeze upon his skin from some unknown source. She touched his thigh, and it was just as good as having real fingers. For all intents and purposes, this was as real as anything else.

"Judging by your videos, you seem to prefer women on the . . . busty side." She said this while looking down at her own flat chest, and her lips made a sad little whimper.

"I do," he said, and it was true.

But then, as if by magic, her breasts began to swell. Chuck watched as they ballooned up, the scrub top and bra underneath making a groaning sound as her body pushed against the material. He felt the heat rush to his face, and Ellie just threw her head back and laughed, hands on hips. Her breasts continued to grow, the buttons popping off, the undershirt riding up to reveal her beautiful, toned stomach. And then, it stopped, and she rocked her hips from side to side to showcase just how firm they'd become.

"Holy shit!" he said, fighting the urge to touch them.

"Go on, you can do it," she said, arching her back and leaning her triple-Ds out toward him.

"Um," he said, hesitating. "I . . . have a girlfriend."

Again, Ellie laughed and cocked her head to the side. "Haven't you ever fantasized about fucking someone who wasn't your girlfriend? This is the same. We aren't cheating here. This is all in your mind, remember?"

He couldn't argue with that logic.

Ellie slipped out of the scrub top. The white undershirt was taut against her breasts, nipples pushing through. And then, she pulled that over her head, and Chuck was left with the largest, most beautiful breasts he'd ever seen. He slid off the bed so that he was closer to them, and then lifted each one in his hands. This may have been a dream, but it certainly felt real. Her breasts were warm and firm, and as he tweaked her nipples, those began to elongate.

"That feels nice," she said, her eyes fluttering closed.

"So you can feel this too?" he wondered.

"Oh definitely. I'm sure my sleeping body is getting wet right about now. Because I sure am."

He leaned down and popped one of her nipples into his mouth, without even asking, and started to suck. Her whole body went limp, and she put a hand up to his shoulder and rubbed, and he forgot all about this being a dream. The rock in his pants was painful as he switched nipples, and when he finally pulled away, she was flustered, standing there topless, her hair pulled behind her back in a clump.

"Can you do the same thing for your ass that you did for your breasts?" he asked.

"Oh honey," she said, smiling. "I can do whatever I want here."

And then she turned around, put her hands to her hips and locked her legs. Her ass was swelling—the material of her pants getting tight and smooth. He couldn't help himself, so he reached out a hand and touched her cheek, feeling it expand under his fingers. Then, Chuck gave it a wallop, a hard smack that made her yelp and dance forward a few steps on her tiptoes. She looked back and smiled and said, "How's that?"

"Make it a little bigger, please?" He was moving up toward her so he could grab a hold of her thighs, and then he shoved his dick (still beneath the jeans) right against her cheeks. It felt amazing to watch them grow out and back toward him, and when it was over, her scrub pants were six-inches shorter and the fabric around her ass had tiny rips in it.

"This whole thing is amazing!" he said. He backed up so she could turn around, which required her to also back up because her breasts had continued to grow a little while her ass was pushing out. She was a new woman now, small but incredibly curvy.

"You like me?" she asked, doing a spin. Her newly enhanced parts jiggled in all the right ways.

"You have no idea. This technology is blowing my mind!" he said.

"Sugar, you haven't seen anything yet. Why don't you get a little more comfortable?" She gently put her fingers in the waistband of his jeans and tugged. Chuck didn't need to be told twice, so he quickly unzipped them and let them fall, his dick now flopping to attention.

She reached down with a warm hand and started to stroke him. Her eyes were on his, her tongue passing by to lick her lips. And then, she pushed forward and kissed him, her giant breasts driving him back against the hospital bed. If not for the giant mounds between the two of them, the kiss would have been more effective, but it was a struggle to find her lips while they were forcing the two apart. Still, she kept her hold on his dick and stroked.

"I think it's only fair that you also get comfortable," he said, looking down at her stressed scrubs.

Ellie simply turned around, bent over, and the pants shred down the middle, her large ass cheeks jiggling out and coming to rest. He took advantage of such a position and pulled her back, resting his dick along the crack of her ass. She made a little sigh, and then bent over again, this time reaching between her legs to grab at his dick. She helped ease him into her pussy, and as soon as he felt that wonderfully warm and wet tunnel, he took her hips and pulled her back toward him. Ellie's body was going limp and he could hear the soft moans leave her lips, so he stood there at the bed, pulling and pushing her, doing all the work. Each time he thrust, her breasts moved out in a wide arc.

And then, something was happening that he couldn't explain, although he was an expert in such things.

His dick kept slipping out, causing either Chuck or Ellie to constantly reposition it. He was trying to hold onto her ass, but he was sure she'd made it start to grow again. Her cheeks were widening out, but they were also . . . rising up. He looked down, and noticed his feet around hers were getting noticeably smaller, and that's when it hit him, and he pulled out—both from shock and because his minuscule dick could no longer hit its mark at such an angle.

She stood up and turned around, and now it was apparent that Chuck was getting smaller. Already the shorter girl was slightly taller than him, a complete reversal from when they'd first started and she had to look down on him. His hand found his dick, slicked with her juices, and started to stroke. Inch by inch, he was shrinking smaller, the beautiful, curvy girl rising up.

"How small am I gonna get?" he asked. His tininess was subtle—he was looking directly at her neck.

"I haven't decided yet. I can make either of us any size I want. But I think for now, I'll keep you at a size that's beneficial to me." And with that, he stopped shrinking, his face directly in front of her breasts. Again she pushed them forward, only this time they were all-encompassing and he had no way to escape. He put his hands up and massaged them, knowing he could fit his head between them if she'd only part them around his ears. He was kissing every inch of her flesh, and as she backed up a little, it allowed him to pop a nipple into his mouth.

He sucked, and noted just how different it felt than it did a few minutes ago when he was normal-sized. She had more force behind it, as well, and each time she pushed forward, he was bent back awkwardly. Chuck wondered for a brief moment if he could be hurt here, or killed. He probably couldn't die in this place, but she could probably cause him physical pain if she wished. It stood to reason if he could sense pleasure, he could also sense pain. And wasn't there a fine line between the two? A line he loved to ride?

When he was finished, she took a step back, her elongated nipples as hard as tacks. Then, she got on her knees, which put her breasts somewhere around his stomach. He was mesmerized by how they bounced, and he wondered if it were possible for his dick to get any harder. Already the veins were popping out painfully along the shaft. She took it in her hand, her fingers looking only slightly bigger than before, and started to stroke.

"What size is he normally?" she asked, not looking up.

"Around seven inches," he said. "Not too bad?"

"Eh," she said, and flashed him a smile. "We can do a little better though."

And then he was feeling heat in the head of his cock. He looked down, braced himself against the hospital bed and watched, amazed, as it grew between Ellie's fingers. It felt amazing to get bigger, as if he were riding the edge to a tremendous orgasm. His head swelled to the size of an apple, and his shaft continued to snake upward, growing both thicker and longer. Her fingers, which were even scaled up larger, couldn't completely close around his member. When it was finished and the tingling and warmth faded, he was sporting a nine-inch cock. He couldn't help himself to touch it, and both hands were able to wrap around the shaft.

"Geez, can I keep this when I wake up?" he asked, jokingly.

"Sorry, sweetheart. You have to turn back into a pumpkin at the stroke of midnight." She left him with that as she descended, putting his entire shaft into her mouth. She licked along it, the veins popping out even more. Ellie's lips parted around the head, her suction threatening to dismember him. He put his hands in her hair, feeling the blond locks curl around his fingers, and that's when he realized that she was changing—or perhaps it was him.

"It's both of us," she said, as if reading his mind. Perhaps she could in this shared world. "We are transferring size. While I grow, you shrink." She then went back to work, making his cock feel better than it had in years.

But she was right. The more she sucked, the smaller he became. The hospital bed was starting to ride up above him, and Ellie twice had to change positions because she had gotten so big that simply sitting on her knees wasn't an adequate position to suck. By the time he was sure their changing had stopped, she was splayed out across the thick carpet, her body looking impossibly long. He stared straight up and realized he couldn't hop back onto the hospital bed even if we wanted.

When she stood up, her height was dizzying. She was now well over his head, and her breasts were so large that he could only see the underside of them. Even her nipples were obscured, not to mention her face. Every now and then he could spot a flash of teeth as she smiled between them, but Ellie had become, in every sense of the word, a giantess. Although their actual sizes were difficult for him to tell, especially with arousal on the forefront of his brain, he guessed he was roughly half her size, perhaps a little smaller. He was having to look slightly upward to face her pussy, although he could reach it if he tried.

"How's this stacking up to your fantasy?" she asked, twirling in a circle. She backed up, pushing his face against the hospital bed with her thick, bulbous ass.

"It's even better," he said once she'd unpinned him.

"That little dick might be supersized, but it's not gonna fill me up now," she said, pointing down. "Best use your mouth."

And before he could agree, she was coming forward, slightly bending at the knees, and pushing her wet pussy right into his face. Her taste and scent were divine, and he dug his nails into the back of her thighs so he could pull himself closer, deeper. She wasn't quite large enough to fit his whole face in, but it was enough. Her pussy felt like his world at that moment, and the more he sloshed his tongue across her lips and over her clit, the wetter she became. Ellie was quite vocal when it came to getting off, and he was surprised how easily it had been, as she was drenching him with each passing second.

"Keep it up little man, I got a few more in me," she said, and then he could feel her weight shift as she leaned over onto the bed. Now, she was just thrusting her hips, and with each one, her pussy smacked him in the face. He loved it, but she was moving too fast to be of any service. However, the job was getting done, as was evident by the steady stream of cum rolling down her legs. When she was finished, she collapsed into the floor, just in front of him. She pulled up a breast and motioned for him to come latch on.

Her hand was stroking his hair and it felt quite odd, as if it were getting bigger. He didn't need to look up, for the nipple was swelling in his mouth but this was such a fantasy that he *had* to see it happen. Chuck let go and watched as the room shot out in all directions. The bed was looking massive now, and he could see beneath it. There were no dust bunnies in this fantasy world. Ellie just sat there watching him dwindle away, her arms resting behind her, large thighs flanking him.

"How small am I getting this time?" he asked. He reached out and put a steadying hand on her big toe, just as he became the same size as her whole foot.

"How small do you think?" she asked, and then spread her legs. "I need you to be a . . . useful size."

He stopped shrinking when he was half the size of her foot. She moved it out of the way and there before him was the largest creature he'd ever seen move. They had both changed size—when he looked back to the bed, he was able to make a quick comparison of it and her body, and realized she was probably pushing twelve feet. That meant he was probably standing at a foot tall or less. But now, as she had said, he was a useful size. Pussy size.

"Guess I'm going in," he said, walking down the valley between her thighs.

"Guess you are," she agreed. "Head first. Be a man."

"Yes, ma'am," he said, and gave a silly, floppy salute before charging right ahead. She leaned back, bit her lip, and readied herself for the tiny man.

He did as she asked and pushed in, face first. It was much different now than it had been a few minutes ago when he was trying to eat her out standing up. Now, she held herself apart and let him easily wiggle his way in. The walls closed in on him, and then the darkness, and he was left by a strangely soft tunnel that was wet and warm. Her scent was all over him, soaking him from head to toe. Somehow, he was still able to breathe—the magic of the Dream Machine.

"Kick around a little," she said, and her voice was clear in his head, as if they were speaking via headset. "Use your arms. Get me off, little man."

He did as the goddess demanded, flipping around back and forth, as he was just the right size to be able to move end over end. Each time she became aroused, the tunnel closed up, tightening around him to the point of cutting off his air. He twirled around, flailing his arms and legs against her soft flesh until she was filling with juices. And then, his body was swelling. It sent a warm shiver down his spine, and he grabbed his dick and started to jerk.

"I'm growing you back just a little bit. I want to really feel your whole body," her voice called out, sounding very discombobulated.

She took his wiggle room away, and now he was using his arms and legs much more effectively. He felt he had a little bit of strength, a little bit of pleasure and pain to his size. And as he thrashed about, he knew the gravity outside was changing because she was bucking off the floor, carrying him into the air with her.

She got off several times, and each one felt like a carnival ride. It was smart making him a little bigger, because each time she orgasmed, her juices shot out, and had he been smaller, he would've been washed away with them. But now, through the magic of the Dream Machine, he was stable and stationary, and wasn't going anywhere until she chose to take him out.

It was like he spent an hour inside her. He tried talking to her, but she wouldn't answer back, or perhaps couldn't. Maybe her method of speaking only worked one way. Still, it was a little disconcerting, and he wondered if there was a problem with the machine. If not for the steady, slightly elevated heartbeat within the walls of her pussy, he would've been worried.

But alas, she started moving again, and her juices came once more. Only now, he felt his inches slipping away, and no more could he perch himself against the walls of her love tunnel. Now, he was sliding across her smooth skin, carried out by her juices. He landed on the thick carpet between her legs, the large mounds of flesh shaking from getting off so many times in a row.

He looked back at her, but still couldn't see her face because of her breasts, only the outline of blond hair around them.

"Care to put me on your tits?" he said, yelling up. "I can't see you anymore."

"Sorry, little guy," she said, and her fingers descended and gently wrapped around his torso. He felt a slight sense of vertigo as she lifted him into the air and deposited him on her left breast. It was bouncy, yet firm. Chuck stared directly ahead to the gargantuan woman, her teeth large enough to bite him in half. She was smiling, and her face was flushed. Ellie tried her best to keep her breathing steady, for if it became too tumultuous, he would go tumbling down her body.

"I thought you'd passed out or something," said Chuck. He got down on his knees and started to rub his hands across her areola. His face buried against her nipple and felt it rise under his lips.

"Sorry fella. I had to step out of the machine for a bit."

He stopped long enough to look up curiously.

"Sorry," she said again. "I know it's all one endless sex session for you, but I've been coming and going inside this dream for almost a year."

"A *year*?" he said, standing up. "I've been unconscious that long?"

"Yes," she said, but smiled gently. "But you're getting better. You have a lot of brain function now. I would say you'll be out of here in the next six months. It won't seem long to you at all."

He went back to work, kissing her nipple while she used a finger to stroke along his back. It felt wonderful, and when she stopped for a moment, he was able to look back and see the twinkle in her eye. The pauses were subtle, like an old VHS tape expertly spliced. It was in those moments that she 'unhooked' from him, and went about her life. This probably happened way more often than he guessed.

"Did you just leave me?" he asked.

"I did. You're almost better. You woke up twice, but I'm sure you don't remember. These little dates will be coming to a close soon."

"These dates? This has been a thirty-minute session for me," he said.

"I know. I'm sorry. It's just . . . I'll miss you."

"I'll miss you too," he said.

He went back to the other breast, sucking on it, pushing his face and hands into it until finally she said, "I have an idea."

"What's that?"

"They're going to take you off the medicine tomorrow, which means you'll wake up. You have a long road ahead of you. Lots of physical and occupational therapy. But I'll help every step of the way."

"I appreciate that. But you said you had an idea?"

"You've made a lot of money in your industry, right?"

"Yeah, I suppose you could say that."

"The experimental wing of my hospital is shut down. They aren't going to fund the Dream Machine anymore. Which means this particular unit will be for sale . . ."

"And I could buy it?"

"And I could visit whenever you want me."

"Just one request," he said, bending back over and massaging her nipple.

"Yes?"

"I get to control our sizes."

"Not so sure I like that idea," she said, lifting him up. "But we'll see. You've got two minutes of 'dream time' left. Make it count." And then, she shoved him back into her wet, waiting pussy.

Short One
No More

If only her mother could see her now. She'd told Beth not to marry Jack on several occasions, but it was hard to see the truth when you were so in love, and your self-worth was so small. And for some reason Beth always thought of her mom, God rest her soul, whenever she was in the shower, sobbing silently. After Jack beat her, this was her only place of solace. Either he didn't care to chase her there, or simply didn't realize she was taking three or four showers a day. In truth, the water made her feel better, and she could gather her thoughts before work in the gentle quiet.

When she stepped out of the shower, and split open the door, he was already sitting at the kitchen table, the newspaper pulled open to hide his face. She was on the verge of a breakthrough in the lab, and she wanted so much for him to be proud of her, to at least acknowledge her hard work, but he wasn't the type to do that. It was no secret that he didn't love her, nor did he care for her. After all these years, it surprised her that it still hurt to make that realization.

"We got the MA calibrated," she told him, gingerly stepping into the kitchen. The MA was the Matter Arranger, and it was going to revolutionize everything. Couldn't he be proud of that? At the very least, he should've been happy to know they'd have money coming their way. She continued. "Nick and Amber ran a test this morning and increased an ear of corn by two-hundred percent. Can you imagine what this'll do for world hunger?"

"Will it help *my* hunger? Because I'm fucking starving. You done?"

She bit her lip, ended her story, and immediately went to fixing his breakfast. Jack was a large guy—seven feet tall—your typical alpha male who didn't take anyone's shit. He was a commanding presence, and everyone in his life cowered before him. It hadn't always been that way, but as he lost sight of his football years and started to feel the 'thirty year spread,' his attitude toward life began to change. Beth had become his punching bag just five years ago, and it was easy because she was miniscule, even by normal-sized standards. She stood just two inches shy of five feet. Thankfully, Jack was smart, and never sent her to the emergency room, although a time or two she thought she needed it. Most of her damage was light bruises and burst lips.

"I'll be late tonight," she said a little while later, shoveling the eggs and bacon from the skillet onto his plate. "Nick wants to show me the new code on the MA and I—"

Jack had wrapped a beefy hand around her arm and held her tight. He flicked the paper back angrily and fixed her with a devilish stare.

"You fuckin' that guy?"

"What? No, of course not. Why would you think that?" she asked. This was a new one.

"You're always working late. Is it just the two of you in that lab?"

"No, Amber's always there too. It isn't like that with Nick at all. He has a girlfriend."

"Oh, so you guys must talk," said Jack, his voice rising. This was never a good thing.

"Of course we talk. We're around each other for twelve hours a day. How could you not know this?"

"So it's my fault, huh?" he said, shoving the plate away.

"No, Jack. That's not what I mean." But she'd already wound up the beast.

He looked at her for a moment longer, those ravenous eyes boring into her soul. When Jack got like this, his anger could go either way—a violent rage or a simmering, at which point it would surface later, all the more potent. Sometimes it was best for him to just get it out and be done with it, no matter how badly it hurt. And as she stood her ground and stared right back, she knew it would certainly hurt badly.

After that, she was on the table, her face painfully slamming against his hot plate of food. He was screaming at her, in his tirade that always burst from the gate the moment the anger flared. She simply waited for it to be over—much the way she did during sex. Jack did what he wanted and Beth was simply along for the ride. He was cursing at her, calling her a whore, a slut, a homewrecker, and even threatened to come to the lab to 'kick the shit' out of that guy Nick. She wept quietly as she often did, and wondered if the stinging in her eyes was blood or tears.

Half an hour later, as she sat in the floor picking up the shattered plate and food, he swept through the house again, a new man, a changed man, a sorry man. He leaned down, kissed her on the cheek and told her that he overreacted and that he'd make it up to her. She just nodded. This late in the game, she was used to such things. In the beginning, when he first started using her face as stress relief, she believed his lies. She believed that he was truly sorry after each time. But now, they were hollow words. He'd never change. And she'd probably never have the courage to leave. Jack told her he loved her one last time before he picked up his briefcase and left for work.

And then, she allowed herself to have a breakdown.

***

She did her best to hide her face with makeup as she entered the lab later that afternoon, but Amber had worked so closely with her for so long, that the girl knew exactly when something was bothering her. And since Beth was so mild-mannered and easy-going, it was no mystery from where her source of contention came. Amber had been a big advocate for divorce ever since the first day Jack laid a hand on her.

"Shit, you need to leave his ass," said Amber a few minutes after she'd arrived. Nick was already at the console, running tests. He tried not to get involved in Beth's personal life, but in truth he probably just didn't know what to say. This was a strange subject, an awful situation, and she was embarrassed having to talk about it.

"One day," she said, smiling weakly. Both knew it would never happen. "So show me the MA."

"Why show you the MA when I can show you results." She pulled the blanket off a table, and beneath it sat an ear of corn that was three-feet long. The kernels were the size of grapes. Beth put hands to her face and laughed, feeling true joy for the first time in weeks.

"You did it," she said, looking at her lab partners.

"We did it," said Nick, pushing his glasses up and running a hand across his smooth head. "All three of us."

"I'd like to see it in action now," said Beth. For the time being, she'd forgotten all about her life, about her abusive husband.

Nick brought the MA around and dropped it into her hand. It looked like a cellphone, although slightly bigger than most current models. It was sleek, black, and looked as if it could be aimed from both ends, but only one side was the emitter and one was the tiny solar array that could help power the fuel cell. Along the top was the input screen—all touch, as these days it was cheaper to implement than actual buttons. The data that came up would confuse all but the smartest cryptologists because it wasn't meant to be user-friendly. It was meant for the in-house researchers only. So the three of them had memorized data sets, and knew exactly what to punch in to make things grow and shrink. And although Beth could operate it with just as much ease as the other two, this was the first time she'd seen it work.

"Have you tried it out on people?" she asked. Amber and Nick just looked at each other and then he quickly pulled it out of her grasp. She stood there dumbfounded as he punched in data and then aimed it right at her. "Whoa, whoa, I don't know about this."

But he wasn't listening. He fired at her, pushing the small recessed button on the base. A bright, green light hit her in the chest and just like that, she was shooting up. Her legs getting thicker, longer. Her arms, fingers, toes—all elongating. It was a quick spurt, only netting her about five or six inches. Now, she was almost as tall Amber. This was the most amazing thing ever.

"Holy shit! We're gonna be rich!" she said, looking down her shirt at her large, plump breasts. "But wait, can it shrink too? Do we have that up and running yet?"

"Silly girl," said Amber. "Think I'd let him grow you if he couldn't fix you back?"

Nick smiled and zapped her again, the five inches bleeding away as if they weren't ever there. A part of her was sad now. It felt good being a little bigger, and there was no nausea or pain accompanied with changing size. However, there was a lot of paperwork. What Nick just did was strictly against the rules, and had anyone from upper management known how they were so callously using the MA, they'd all be in trouble, and most likely lose their funding and their lab.

"We even added a self-administering setting this morning," said Nick. He handed it back to Beth, showed her how to operate it and then let her try it for herself.

She pressed the button and felt a small jolt run through her body, and then she was shooting up again, a few inches past Amber. The device seemed to scale along with her, which was handy. Her friends had made a lot of improvements in the short time she'd been away.

"Holy shit, I'm a giant!" said Beth, looking at her friends who now came up to her chest.

"Nah," said Amber. "You're taller than us, but you're not a giant. You should've seen Nick earlier. He made himself twenty feet tall."

"Seriously?" Beth asked. "What was that like?"

Nick looked at Amber nervously, as if he was afraid to answer, but Beth quickly realized it was only because the answer was a secret—or perhaps a little naughty.

"What did you two do?" she asked Amber, mouth wide, but a smile was beginning to form.

Both her lab partners were quiet for a moment and then Amber finally blurted out, "Oh, God Beth. He has the biggest dick. I mean right now, normal-sized, his dick is *huge*. Like nine and a half inches, right Nick?"

"Uh . . . yeah." He'd started to rub a hand across his bald head, his cheeks flushing.

"So I thought, 'wow, Nick, can I see it? Now that you're twenty feet tall?'"

Beth felt her own skin flushing and it wasn't lost on her that Nick was starting to pitch a tent in his pants.

"And did he show you?" Beth asked.

"Oh yeah. Damn thing was like a tree trunk. It was so warm and so . . ."

"That's enough, Amber," said Nick, only because he was growing embarrassed.

"No, I wanna hear," said Beth. "His dick was so what?"

Amber grinned. "So hard."

"I stroked it for her," said Nick, loosening up a little.

"Yeah, cause I couldn't do it. I tried and my hands barely went around it."

"I'm sure that was nice," said Beth.

"It was okay," said Nick. "No payoff, though."

"Well of course not, silly," said Amber. "We can't have your dick shooting its load in here while you're twenty feet tall!"

"True," said Nick. "But maybe one day. Maybe one day we can both get big and have fun."

"I'd totally be up for that," said Amber.

"Hello? I'm still here," Beth said, then reverted back to her normal size.

"Yes you are," said Nick. "Sorry, we got carried away."

"It's okay. That's really cool, though. I'm happy for you guys. That's a really fun way to use the MA. I wish I had that chance."

"Yeah, well you're married to a grade-A asshole," said Amber flatly. Nick saw himself out of the conversation and sat back down at his workstation.

"This is true."

"But you know. . ." Amber said, her voice trailing off as she became lost in thought.

"Yes?" Beth said.

"You could finally turn the tables on that gargantuan bastard," Amber said.

"That would be risky," said Beth, although she'd thought the same thing many times.

Again, Amber looked lost in thought, but then she stood up and pulled Beth out of the lab and said, "Come with me. I want to show you something."

She led her back into the offices where administration worked but they had all gone to lunch. Amber and Beth both shared a workspace, an area next to the lab where they maintained their important paperwork—grants and funding sources mostly. But Amber sat at her desk and pulled out a lockbox, then flipped open the lid. She produced another MA, this one looking strikingly similar to the one Beth had just held, only this one was white and a tiny bit larger.

"You built another one? How?" asked Beth.

"Because we had extra funding that was off the books. Don't worry about it. But I've been keeping it updated in line with our prototype. I wanted this one . . . because I want to have a little fun with Nick. We've talked about shrinking and growing so much and once the MA leaves the lab for further testing and marketing, I wanted to make sure we kept one. And now I'm going to let you borrow it."

"Me?"

"Yes. Go even the odds with your fucking Viking. I won't tell a soul if you won't."

Beth's fingers were shaky as she reached out and took it, not knowing how she would use it, or even if she would. But the thought filled her with such joy, and she would give it a go, nonetheless.

"Thank you," said Beth, taking it. "I don't really know what to say."

Amber smiled and leaned back in her seat. "Say you'll make that son of a bitch sorry for hitting you."

***

As she looked into the mirror that evening, Beth had already made an important decision—she'd never be short again. She pulled out the MA and dialed up her intended height and pressed the button. Instantly she felt flushed, her skin growing warm, and she began to inch taller. This build of the device went a little slower, but that was fine. It still provided the same results. She grew until she was six-feet tall, more than a foot bigger than her normal size. She wondered how long, if ever, it would take Jack to notice. He certainly didn't notice when she bought a new outfit or cut her hair.

She was sitting at the kitchen table, reading a magazine and drinking a Diet Coke when he lumbered in. It was always obvious what kind of day he'd had by the way he threw his keys and briefcase into the corner by the door. Also by the way his necktie hung loosely around his collar. Today must not have been a good one, for he ran his hands through his sweaty hair and then fixed her with a curious eye from down the hall. By now, she usually had his dinner prepared but she hadn't even started it. He came into the kitchen and looked first to the empty stovetop, and then to her.

"Where's dinner?" he asked.

"I didn't make it. I thought maybe you could make us something tonight."

"Is this a fucking joke? I'm not in the mood, Beth."

"It's not a joke," she said, and then stood up. He was still bigger by a foot, but he was nowhere near as imposing. He just looked at her, obviously thrown off by her way of talking to him. She'd never stood up to him before, but it didn't seem as if he noticed that she was closer to his size.

"What the hell, Beth." He came around the table, but she took a step back, which was also out of character for her. Normally, she'd just take her punishment and be done with it. But because she retreated, he stopped and considered her. That gave her plenty of time to pull the MA from her pocket and point it at him. His face nearly broke into laughter—she could see the smile pulling at his lips. "What's that?"

"Let's call it an attitude adjuster," she said. And while he was contemplating her words, she turned it toward him and hit the activation button. The green light shot out so fast and blasted him in the chest that he didn't have time to jump out of the way. And then, as the green quickly spread across his body and dissipated, he found himself backing away again, swatting at the tendrils of light that were no loner there. He was angrier at her, but he didn't know why—he didn't understand what had just happened.

And then, Jack began to shrink.

It wasn't much—just a foot, which landed him at an even six feet tall. He was still a big guy, but she was also a big girl. She'd completely leveled their height and now it was unmistakable. Now, he had no choice but to see it.

"Fuck . . . did I just . . . shrink?" He wasn't necessarily talking to her—he was looking around the room, amazed by the slight change in his environment. But he quickly noticed Beth again once she spoke up.

"Yep. I just made you a foot shorter. Oh, and in case you didn't notice because you're a complete asshole, I was already a foot taller. Guess what, babe? We're the same size now!"

He was shaking now, and of course she was afraid. Jack was very much a threat because he was corded in muscles. A six-foot man was still a force to be reckoned with. She found herself backing toward the oven, but he was on her in a flash, ripping the MA from her fingers. She tried to fight at him, but he easily held her back at an arm's length.

"Stop it!" she said. "You don't know what you're doing!"

"How does this thing work? Can I make myself bigger?"

He was pushing buttons. She could hear the beeps and had no idea how the device was being set. Jack was horrible with technology, but she knew this was probably bad. And then, the bright green light left the end and shot her right in the face. She spit, as if it was something tangible that had gone into her mouth, but that notion was silly. How the hell was she ever going to survive if she became smaller again?

But that's not what was happening.

Jack's scowl was getting further away because she was growing. In his mindless button-mashing he'd reset the device for growth, and now he was slowly backing away, looking down at the MA in his hands. He wanted to try again, but knew his own limitations with gadgets. Jack was sure that if he fired, it would just make things worse. Beth continued to shoot upward, passing the seven-foot mark, then the eight-foot, nine-foot, and finally her growth stopped at around ten feet tall, just below the ceiling fan. He was looking rather miniscule now, and he stared up at her with tears in her eyes.

Her breasts were so large, so thick, that she couldn't even see him until he took a few steps back. Her hands found her hips and she threw her head back and laughed. It was enough to rattle the windows over the sink.

"Babe, just calm down," he said, retreating another step. She was worried he'd dart out of the house and she might not be fast or agile enough to chase him.

She rushed him, putting hands on his shoulders and throwing him against the kitchen counter. At the same time, she was rotating around so that he couldn't go through the doorway. He was afraid—his little arms were shaking and tears were streaming down his face. He knew how he'd treated her all these years, and it was time for a little payback. Beth bent down and snatched the MA from his fingers. He just looked on blankly, as if he wasn't even aware he'd been holding it.

Then, she reprogrammed it and aimed it toward him, savoring his reaction as he sank to his knees and said, "Please, babe. Please don't zap me. I'll be good."

"You don't know how to be good. And I'm done taking orders from you."

She pulled the trigger.

He screamed out as he suddenly began to dwindle down. Jack's first impulse was to run but she grabbed him around the throat and held him still. She could feel his flesh slipping between her fingers as he grew smaller and smaller. His eyes were wide as the world changed around him, most notably his wife who was quickly becoming double his size. Finally, he reached a height of four feet tall, barely able to reach across the kitchen counters. But to a ten-foot woman, he appeared much smaller, only coming up to her thighs.

Jack looked around, for the world to him had severely changed. This was a guy who normally stood at seven feet tall, who took shit from no one, who was an athlete and could do many great things. Now, he was reduced to the size of a child, unable to even get a glass of water without a stepladder. Beth moved closer to him, his head resting painfully against the countertop. He was crying, but he was also trying to hide it. Jack had always been a proud man.

"Let's go. I have a job for you," she said, taking him by the wrist and dragging him toward the bedroom. He tried to fight her, to dig in his heels, but she aimed the MA at him again and he simply fell apart and let her take him through the house.

When they made it into the bedroom, she sat on the edge of the bed where she ripped off his clothes, no matter how painful. She popped the buttons, shredded the belt and the pant legs, and finally jerked the shoes off until there was a tiny, naked man. He was holding himself, as if he didn't want her to see his shrunken dick.

While he stood there shivering, she undressed herself, her large breasts falling out of her shirt once the bra was off. She had a beautiful, shaved pussy, which was now so big that no dick on Earth could satisfy it. No matter. She didn't want his dick, not anymore. But that didn't mean he still wasn't useful.

"Eat me," she said, spreading her legs. From the way she sat, it was simply a walk-up to him. He could approach and lean in and get to work.

"Fuck you," he said, but regretted it instantly. She brought a hand down hard on his head, to which he took a knee and started to sob.

"Want to try again?"

He stood up, started to approach her pussy, but she was bored with how long he was taking. She snatched him around the back of his head and pushed him in, his whole face rubbing against her lips. Jack said something, made a moan and whimper, but she didn't care, nor did she acknowledge. She kept a firm hand to coax him to continue working.

She came over and over, but not because of his work—it was because of hers. He was simply a sextoy that she maneuvered however she saw fit. Jack had to be soaked because her fingers were, as well as his hair. Every few minutes she had to relax a little so he could pull away and catch his breath. It was rather comical—her shrunken husband, her cum all over his face, dripping down his chin, and sucking in air like a beached fish. But once he made eye-contact with her, it was back to work. Her hand swiftly pushed him back into her warm and wet and waiting pussy.

They played this game well into the evening, until she decided she wanted to change it up a little and made a larger size difference between them. Beth set the device to self-administer and added two more feet to her height, the bed starting to sag in the middle. This brought her to twelve feet long, spread across the bed with her knees up high. The tiny man eating her out was now roughly a third of her size, and she could push his whole head into her, although she did this sparingly because he had to take so long to recover afterwards.

He tried to run so many times because her hold was slipping now that he was smaller. But on the last attempt of wrangling him, she decided to teach him a lesson. She shrank him again, this time really small—and when she picked him up between her fingers, he was screaming, so huge her face looked. She shoved him into her pussy and then put on her tight panties so he couldn't get out. And then, she fell asleep with him inside her.

The next morning she awoke and pulled him out. He had been asleep too, and somehow had managed not to run out of air. She was sure that when she went to retrieve her tiny husband he'd be a small, shriveled mess. But no, he coughed her cum from his mouth and used his weak arms to pick himself back up.

"Morning, sleepy!" she said, her voice so loud and forceful that it knocked him over.

"Shit," he said, looking dejected.

"Aww, did my little husband think it was all a dream?" she said, and laughed.

He shook his head and dropped it to his lap. "I'm sorry," he said weakly. "I'm sorry for all I've done."

"I'm sure you are," she said, not fazed by his ever-insistent apologies. "But you have a lot of work to do in order to make it up to me."

He didn't have a reply for that. Perhaps he thought it best just to remain quiet.

She placed him on the floor and then zapped him. His face immediately went pale, fearful that he was getting even smaller (where to now, between her toes?) but this faded when his size began to return. Slowly, he inched bigger, until he stood at four feet tall, just like yesterday. He looked up at Beth with dawning understanding, and perhaps a bit of irritation.

"What?" she said, shrugging her shoulders. "You didn't think I'd make you normal again, did you? You've got to earn your inches. And I'll be honest with you, love . . . I don't think you'll ever be seven feet again."

He dropped his head once more, his shoulders heaving.

Just then, the doorbell rang. His eyes lit up, as if this were someone here to rescue him, but she'd already checked her messages this morning and knew firsthand that it was not. He looked back at her quizzically.

"Go answer it," she said, nodding toward the hallway.

"Really?" He looked down at himself. On one hand, he was four feet tall. On the other, he was completely naked.

"Yep. Go. Don't make me zap you."

He turned around, rushed toward the door and she couldn't help but watch him as he struggled to reach the handle and pull it open. The tiny, naked man fell back after seeing what was standing on the porch.

It was a giant pair of legs and a crotch.

Amber leaned down so she could clear the doorway and entered. "Hey there, little guy!" she said, her voice projecting all through the house. "I heard you've been misbehaving."

He crawled backwards out of her reach and then ran back to the bedroom, as if he would be safe from the other giantess. Now, he was stuck in a house at four feet tall, trapped between two twelve-foot tall women.

"Hello, love," said Beth. "Good of you to come."

"I couldn't pass up an opportunity like this. You look gorgeous. Look at those tits." Beth pushed them together and held them out.

"Have you seen my ass?" She twirled around, showing her bulbous cheeks.

"Why is she here?" asked Jack from the corner. He'd squeezed himself between the cabinets.

Amber answered. "I'm here because I heard you're an awesome little pussy eater."

He gulped and looked at Beth.

"Oh he is," his wife said. "And if he gives you trouble, you just shrink him down to dildo size."

Amber came on into the house, shedding her clothes as she did. "Really? Then I sure hope he gives me trouble."

Beth pulled him from between the cabinets and picked him up over her shoulder. She carried him into the bedroom where Amber had already gone and found a spot on the bed. She was completely naked. Beth took a seat next to her, and now Jack was staring at two giant pussies.

"Pick, little man," said Beth.

Immediately he rushed toward Amber and buried his face between her legs. She made a tiny sigh, unaware that it would feel so good. "My, my, this is nice." She lay back and spread her arms up the wall.

They spent the whole morning that way, fucking each other—taking turns and joining the little man between the other's legs, and finally shrinking Jack down to sextoy size (even though he'd been good) and scissoring their pussies around him. It was a delicate act that caused them to break the bed, but at least they didn't snap their sextoy. When it was over, they looked down at him, a minuscule piece of meat that was half-whimpering, half sleeping through exhaustion.

"I guess he'll never hit another girl again, will he?" said Amber.

"Nope. He's learned his lesson."

"So what now? Will you make him big? Divorce him?"

"Neither," she said. "Let's go shopping. I need to run somewhere to get him a home."

"A home?"

"Yeah. I'm thinking PetSmart will have what I need."

"Oh girl," said Amber, laughing. "You're bad. But I *love* it."

Back to Basics

The Follow-Up Story to
Back to Nature

"I hate when the stuff wears off," said Mandy, allowing Christina to continue fixing her collar while they rode the elevator. Angelica giggled, looking into her compact so that she could run a hand through her own teased hair. It was the first time in a year that the three had looked presentable—at least by business standards. Mandy hadn't even been in shoes for the last eighteen months, and that morning when she slipped them on, it was almost like learning to walk again.

Angelica said, "We have to blend in if we're to make any sort of impact. They can't see the end result until it's too late."

"She's right," said Christina. "But damn, did we have to wear pantyhose? This thing is driving me crazy!" She reached down and pulled at the material between her legs.

Their company *The Howling Sisters* had really taken off in the last six months. At first, they were a simple dispensary, but that evolved into something so much grander. Mandy's growers had stumbled upon a very particular crop while breeding plants in South America, and the results had been nothing short of amazing. Now, that crop was the hallmark of many products, from special blends, to incense, to lip balm, lotions, and scented candles. Now, The Howling Sisters was on track to make almost half a billion dollars this year alone.

The elevator doors opened, and out stepped three beautiful women, certainly by professional standards. No excess body hair, no long legs, no giantesses—just three ordinary ladies who were set to find new investors in a whole new way. Looking across the room, to the multitude of girls wandering by in their little skirts and pleated dresses and Starbucks cups and high heels—Mandy knew this place was ripe for the picking.

She turned to her companions and said, "Ladies. We all have a job to do. I'll see you shortly." She pulled her rolling suitcase down the hall, looking for Conference Hall F. The entire floor was the size of an amphitheater, with one large room, Conference Hall A, and several medium sized ones for individual presentations. Mandy guessed there to be some two-hundred women here, all from various walks of life, but mostly curtailed by the beauty and entertainment industries. That certainly explained why there was no shortage of young, stunningly beautiful women milling about everywhere she looked.

A woman approached her just outside of Conference Hall F, and when she spoke, Mandy recognized her voice, as they'd spoken several times over the last month by phone. It was Tabitha—the CEO of *LadyWyk Candles*.

"How we doin, lady?" said Tabitha. She was a head taller than Mandy, but such things didn't matter, especially once the product samples began. "I'm very interested in your presentation."

"I'll try to make it a good one. I'm sure everyone is gonna want to take one of these home with them."

"Don't be too cocky," she said. "The majority of the women here didn't even want to come."

"They'll be glad they did."

"I didn't catch the product line. Have you started the marketing yet?" Tabitha asked.

"Not yet," said Mandy, then she smiled. "And it's called Inner Beast."

***

Kaitlyn hated these business trips. If not for the free food, the nice room, and, secretly, the free porn on the television, she wouldn't even bother. Her boss made her do these things, citing that it would build character, get her out from behind a desk, and help her to cultivate relationships. That was all bullshit. Carol hated her, plain and simple. It was a small consolation that her boss also came, for if Kaitlyn had to be miserable and put up with these people, so too did Carol.

Both of them were here to represent *New Girl*, a company that sold clothing and accessories. For some reason they were about to sit in on a demonstration for a special kind of lotion. Lotion? That didn't make sense, and when she brought it up to Carol, the hag simply said that it was the company's decision to make a little dongle to hang from their purses, and in it, some sort of designer lotion. Kaitlyn couldn't think of a more boring way to spend a weekend, but she'd best come to terms with it.

"There they are," said Carol, stepping up and whispering in Kaitlyn's ear. Her boss was a short, squat lady—uptight to the max, with a bun of hair kept tight with several metal pins. She was pointing to the elevator, to where a trio of uncomfortable looking women stepped out and surveyed the room with curious eyes.

"They don't look like much," said Kaitlyn, not caring one bit, but yet she found all three of them rather attractive. Kaitlyn leaned more toward women these days, although she would never tell her boss that. Carol had lived with a girlfriend for years, and Kaitlyn didn't like the idea of finding common ground with the woman.

"Their products are apparently amazing. But not much is known. They're about to become publicly traded. We need to get in there and make a good impression and hopefully get on the buy list."

"You're pretty certain this stuff is good," said Kaitlyn. "Look at that one. She can barely stand up in her heels. These people are frauds."

Carol gave her a chastising look. "They're not frauds. Can I trust you to sit in on this conference? I'll be in the incense one. I'm guessing all three girls will be giving presentation and then we'll have a meet-and-greet for everyone."

"Whatever, Carol. I'll take care of it."

"Watch the attitude. And stand up straight. You're representing a prominent company."

That lost its Fortune 500 status twelve years ago, she thought but did not say.

Kaitlyn wandered around for a few minutes, knowing the conferences were not ready to start for another fifteen minutes. This place was packed, and she hated being around so many uptight women. If they opened a bar over in Conference Hall A, these women would certainly behave differently. Kaitlyn herself wished for a drink, but that wasn't happening. For now, she knew she had to mingle, be pleasant, and then get the hell out of there. What could be more fun than listening to a presentation on lotion?

Inside the conference room, a woman who called herself Christina was setting up a PowerPoint presentation while another woman handed out tiny green bottles of lotion. Kaitlyn didn't care about any of this, but if the lotion would drown out the stench of a dozen businesswomen's perfume, then she would certainly give it a try.

"Morning, ladies," said Christina from the front. "Who's ready to let out their inner beast?"

No one said a thing. There was only the sound of paper folding and a stifled cough. It brought a smile to Kaitlyn's face. Every other woman seated across from her was a carbon copy of the last—terse lips, folded arms, business suit. And here they all were, listening to a woman ready to drone on about lotion.

"In front of you is a sample of our newest lotion in the Inner Beast line—it's called Stubble."

"Not a very sexy name," said Kaitlyn under her breath, but when she popped open the cap and took a whiff, she was pleasantly surprised. It reminded her of the weed she used to smoke in college—the kind that her dealer would cut with something odd, like lavender or basil, just to give it an earthy, fragrant smell. And whether it was the recall of nice memories of that, or she was genuinely into the scent, she couldn't tell.

A woman in the row in front of Kaitlyn turned to her neighbor. "These women actually booked the whole Raleigh Hills Conference Arena for this?" She giggled, as did the girl to whom she was speaking.

"For lotion! I can't believe we're listen to a presentation about lotion! These ladies must have more money than they know what to do with."

"I'm not buying this garbage," said the first girl, sniffing the tiny drop on her thumb.

"Me either, but I'll be polite and listen."

Kaitlyn squeezed out a dab of the viscous, greenish lotion onto her palm and then swirled it around. The other women were doing the same, and she could tell the atmosphere in the room had changed—the women were slightly relaxing, although it was barely noticeable. So far, the Howling Sister in front was staying afloat in her initial presentation. Kaitlyn rubbed her hands together, and it was like liquid gold between them. There was no grittiness to the product, and it was as smooth as a bowling ball. Following in the footsteps of several ladies to her left and right, Kaitlyn took off her suit jacket and rubbed the lotion up her arms. When it ran dry, she dabbed more into her palms and did the same thing again.

"Let your hair down, ladies," said Christina, and when she pulled the pin from her own, a giant cascade of blond locks fell to her shoulders. It was a little off-putting in the situation, but Kaitlyn found her attractive, nonetheless. "We are at a retreat, we are out of the office, and for the most part, our bosses aren't here, right?"

A slow, murmur of agreeing.

"So let's implement a rule right now: What happens in the conference room, stays in the conference room."

Again, a giggle of agreement.

Kaitlyn loved the feeling of the lotion on her skin so much that when she was sure all eyes were on Christina, she took her shoes off, danced out of her pantyhose, and then rubbed some on her legs. It was making her whole body warm, which she couldn't explain. Perhaps it was just the sensation of the cool lotion, perhaps it was the scent, or maybe it was even the fact that she was lowering her inhibitions. Either way, she noticed the other women in the room feeling the same way.

"My feet," a girl said just next to her—a tall, leggy blond beauty. She'd pulled her foot up into her lap and was rubbing a hand across the sole. "They're . . . tingling."

"Yeah," said Kaitlyn, and now that the girl had mentioned it, so were hers. It was barely noticeable at first, just little pinpricks, a tiny increase to sensitivity. But as Kaitlyn rubbed a hand across them, it was like a fire had ignited, and they were so tingly that she wanted to stand. She was feeling quite flushed, and everyone else seemed to feel the same.

Christina, at the front, had already lathered her own arms and legs with the lotion, taking a seat so that she could smear it on her feet, as well. She was smiling at the room, at the ladies' sudden discomfort and curiosity. But then she fixed Kaitlyn with a warm, knowing smile and said, "Now let's have some fun, shall we? Turn to your partner and help rub that lotion into her feet."

"Seriously?" said Kaitlyn, to no one in particular. But the whole room was going along with the presentation. Already women across the table had thrown their feet into their neighbor's lap, and just as Kaitlyn was about to remark on the absurdity of it all, a pair large, size ten feet plopped down on her legs. She looked up to her neighbor, a cheery Asian girl who was grinning ear to ear.

"I'll get it started for you," she said, then squeezed the lotion on her toes.

Kaitlyn put her hands on the lady's warm feet and began massaging the lotion into her soles. The Asian girl lay back in the chair, almost falling asleep. When it was over, she reciprocated, and rubbed lotion into Kaitlyn's feet. It felt wonderful, and the tingling started all over again. She wondered if it would last . . . Without even realizing it, she brought up a hand and adjusted her top, then started scratching an inch that appeared out of nowhere—on her neck, her arms and her face.

***

Down the hall, in a conference room that was smelling just as good, with just as many confused ladies, stood Mandy, lighting the remaining candles around the room. She'd just finished her presentation—had just laid out her financial successes and woes for the products. Each lady had one of the candles in front of her, different scents but all with the trademarked Wild Woman crop blended into the wax. The place was smelling divine, but the aroma was the least impressive attribute of the product lines, as the women here (as well as the other two conference rooms) were about to learn firsthand.

Tabitha was looking especially agitated, but that was to be expected. She was a rather unpleasant woman over the phone, so Mandy assumed she'd just as abrasive in person. Her nose crinkled at the minty scent of the candle in front of her, and she pushed it away. With her arms folded over, she inspected the women to the left and right. Some were hard sells—equally displeased with the product before them, while some were visibly enjoying them. The flames flickered and small tendrils of smoke rose into the air.

"What's wrong, girl?" said Mandy, moving just in front of Tabitha. She'd outlined the different scent profiles and had come back toward her podium. "Not your flavor? We can try others."

"I just don't think this line is for me."

"I'm sorry to hear that." Mandy turned her attention to the others. "Ladies, take your shoes off. I want to try an experiment."

The girls looked at one another curiously, but some were already a little more relaxed than Tabitha, so they did as she asked. At least twenty beautiful women filled the conference hall, and at least twenty pairs of shoes—pumps, flats, heels—began to unfasten while feet began to slip out. Tabitha, seeing how warm the reception to Mandy's request had been, did the same, placing her shoes on the table next to her.

"Everyone stand up." Mandy kicked out of her own shoes and moved to the center of the room so all could see her. "Feel that? You are connected with the Earth. Sure, we're inside a conference center but we are closer to nature right now than we ever get in the city." As she said this, the room became hazy as the candles had begun to permeate the air, far more than what was normal for regular, everyday aromatherapy ones.

And then, they began to notice the change.

At first it was subtle, but the shorter girls in the crowd knew something was different. They were getting taller, their legs lengthening, their toes getting thicker and wider. The sensitivity in their feet was incredible, the very first side-effect of the Wild Woman crop. Mandy was feeling all of these things, and she was so happy to be 'under the spell' again, for wearing normal clothes, being normal-sized, and having normal hair was troublesome.

Tabitha looked at her hands, and quickly she began to pull off her rings and place them inside her shoe. She was inching taller, slowly, her face looking red as her breasts began to press against the buttons on her blouse. A tiny smile cracked the edges of her lips, but she wouldn't allow it—not yet anyway.

Tiny groans erupted throughout the room as dresses and business suits started to shred. No one was shooting up to full-height—it was a slow burn that Mandy orchestrated on purpose. Sure, the weed could be tailored to make someone instantly gigantic, but where was the fun in that?

Several of the girls weren't paying attention to the growing, at least not of their bodies. Instead, they were still seated with their feet propped up on the tables, toes inching taller, soles inching thicker. They were rubbing them, giggling, and at last the Wild Woman crop in the candles had begun to take effect—as one of the most pleasurable parts was a sense of euphoria. They were calm, happy.

"Oh gosh, my feet!" said one girl, a dark-skinned beauty who was about five feet tall when she entered the room but now, with the way her blouse was ripping at the sleeves, was probably closer to seven. "So tingly. And look . . . so big!"

"That's nothing," said the girl next to her, a redhead with freckles peppered across her cheeks. "Look at mine." She brought her feet closer to the dark-skinned girl's, and it was clear that Red's were almost double. Still, by the end of the presentation, who was to say who'd be the biggest?

"Jesus, this is a five-hundred-dollar suit!" said one growing woman from the back, her sleeves ripping.

Red said, "Yeah, I know what you mean." She held up her blouse jacket and said, "Three-hundred bucks for this one. Tailor-made!"

Mandy said, "Don't worry, ladies. You will either be compensated by our tailoring services or I'll buy you all a new wardrobe." That seemed to satisfy the women.

She looked across the room, to the phase one of Wild Woman crop, and noticed a couple girls had fingers inching down toward their sweet spots. This was the reaction she'd hoped for, and by the end of the day, more than one girl would shuck off the business persona, and embrace their inner beast.

***

Kaitlyn was feeling relaxed and she didn't quite understand it because she'd been anything but only twenty minutes ago. But it wasn't relegated just to her—nearly every woman in the room was leaning back, some with their legs on the table while others put their feet in empty chairs. Even Kaitlyn had noticed an intense tingling in her soles, and she was leaned over, face almost resting on the table, rubbing her thumbs across them.

Christina had likewise taken her shoes off, dropping down a few inches in height. The smell of the lotion was permeating the room, and she'd just given a speech about how the products were all-natural and helped them connect with nature, hence the name inner beast. It brought up thoughts of bears and wolves that Kaitlyn found a little silly, but the more her mind eased, the more she became onboard with what the Howling Sisters were selling. And that's when she noticed the subtle changes in her body.

She was about to apply another small glob of the wonderfully smelling lotion when she noticed it wasn't spreading so easily on her arms. And when she looked down, she saw it was matted in hair—subtle little sprouts that were unevenly breaking through her skin. It was all painfully itchy, and as her fingers began to scrape at her arms, legs, neck and face, she realized that many of the other girls were doing the same thing.

A girl across the room—one with close-cut bangs and a bit of a bob—now had noticeably longer and shaggier hair. She certainly didn't look that way when she came in and sat down. And as Kaitlyn stared at her, the girl brought a hand up, tipped in beautifully manicured nails, and started digging into her scalp, as if she had a terrible itch.

Even Christina up front had shed her jacket and blouse, and was now unashamedly in only bra and slacks. When she reached up to scratch her armpit, Kaitlyn noticed a small tuft of hair that made her wonder if it had been there before . . . or was completely new. Kaitlyn's armpits were starting to itch, but that could've only been suggestive. Still, her whole body was itching, her legs were tingling, and suddenly . . . she could feel the hair down below.

Kaitlyn made it a point to stay shaven—most of the girl partners she had preferred it that way, but just now she knew that wasn't the case. There was a snag on her panties, and although she was a little embarrassed, she still reached a hand below. Her fingertips graced a stubble, something that wasn't there before this presentation had begun. Somehow, the lotion was causing her to grow hair and, oddly enough, she didn't care. She was starting to relax, and she forgot all about Carol in the next room over.

"It's okay," said Christina, noticing that Kaitlyn was about to withdraw her hand. "You can masturbate all you want." She leaned in and whispered, "There's a few others doing it already." Kaitlyn flashed a quick glance around the room and realized that it was true. At least four girls were pleasuring themselves, clothing now shed, hair starting to sprout along their arms and legs in uneven tufts.

"Oh, God, I can't believe I'm doing this. I'm so embarrassed." But even still, her hands were reaching down, and just as her fingers found their mark, her pubic hair sprouted up and seemed to twist around them. She was growing wet, and the wetter she became, the more hair seemed to rise along her flesh. Her outstretched toes even had tiny sprouts of hair on them—not much, but subtly there.

As she watched Christina—who was having fun watching *her*—she noticed little tendrils of hair coming up along the Howling Sister's arms and legs. It was a turn on that propelled her to be more aggressive with herself.

"Tell me about it," said Christina. "How does it feel? Are you letting go? Are you . . . embracing your inner beast?"

Kaitlyn didn't have an answer for that, only a smile. She quickened her pace and took another look around the room. By now, the ladies' hair atop their heads had started to lengthen, to roll down past shoulders and backs. Kaitlyn's own was draped across her front, and she'd barely noticed that her breasts were starting to push the bra out. There was so much happening, so much stimulus to her body, that she didn't know what was a part of this odd transformation and what was simply built up in her orgasm-addled brain.

But then, as her fingers came away dripping, she made another odd discovery. The hem of her pants was a little tighter—and she had to rip them in order to withdraw her hand. And then, with her feet on the table, and

Christina's now joined, she watched as her toes got longer, thickened. Christina's soles looked tough, and just seeing them made Kaitlyn's own feet start to tingle all over again.

"Are we . . . *growing*?" she asked. She looked around, feeling her face flush. And then, as if some instinctual beast had clawed its way up her throat, she let out a long, sustained howl. When it was over, she looked around, face turning red. The other girls were giggling and she looked back at Christina for support. "Am I turning into a wolf?"

The Howling Sister laughed. "No, sweetheart. But it's normal to think that."

***

Back inside Mandy's conference room, the ladies knew all about such growth, but the sprouting of hair was just beginning. As she looked across the expanse of tables to the towering beauties, she couldn't help but feel proud that she'd made this happen. Currently there were almost twenty women before her, ranging in heights between nine and twelve feet tall. Tabitha had been the slowest to grow, but such inequalities could happen. The Wild Woman crop was unpredictable, and while the end result was always the same, the trip to getting there was as varied as the highways into the city.

"You know, I didn't want to come today," said Tabitha, resting her tingly feet on the chair next to her. Already, the chair was rolling away, moving off due to the woman's growing.

"I know," said Mandy. She was already nearing her final height, clothes shredded around her ankles. She sat in the undersized desk chair, fingers between her legs . . . waiting for the next phase.

"My sister made me come. Said she'd tried this stuff at a retreat a few months ago but wouldn't tell me anything about it. I was so pissed. You know, to come all the way out here on a whim?" She was moaning a little, her fingers reaching down into her mangled panties.

"And are you glad now?" asked Mandy. She couldn't help but look at the other girls as they stretched out, some writhing on the floor, their legs elongating, feet get thicker and wider. The tables were a mess now—all pushed aside by growing flesh. It was a wonder none of the candles had been tipped over.

"I suppose so," she said, her voice indifferent, but Mandy knew better. The woman's fingers were drenched. "My sis is a whole different lady now. She let her hair grow out. She dresses far more casually and she's been barefoot every time I've seen her lately. And now I guess I know why."

After that, phase two began, and as Tabitha sat there with an odd look on her face, fingers still stuffed below, Mandy knew why.

"Did you get a handful you weren't expecting?" she said, giggling. The pubic hair was coming first, as it always did when the hair phase began. Mandy could feel her own starting to poke at the panties.

"Mmm, that's quite nice," said Tabitha. She pulled out the hem and looked below.

Another woman, a ten-foot beauty named Ruth stood up, her teased hair nearly brushing the ceiling. "Holy hell! Look, you guys!" She grabbed her already shredding underwear and ripped them apart, showing a large, thick bush of hair. The other girls were amazed by it, but this didn't last long because they all became afflicted with the same thing—Mandy was enamored to see them all ripping through whatever remained of their clothes so that they could see their own bushes sprouting—like dandelions after a heavy rain. Mandy joined in and became naked, as well.

Tabitha ran a hand across her face and felt a tiny stubble of hair. She pulled her hand away, horrified because she certainly didn't want a beard. It was a small tuft of hair, barely noticeable if not for feeling it against her palm.

"It's okay," said Mandy. "Totally fine."

Tabitha calmed a little at that.

Now, the rest of the girls were loosening up, and a few of them—those that could do so without banging their heads—joined hands and started to dance around. Tabitha looked at them with a mix of enthrallment and envy, for Mandy could look at her and tell that this was a life she'd never had, but always wanted. Some girls just didn't know how to 'let their hair down' and it was one of the reasons why Mandy had worked so hard to get the Wild Woman crop on the market. She stood up, started to dance, and grabbed Tabitha by the hand, just in time to notice both their arms were spotted with tufts of hair.

"Are you familiar with grounding?" asked Mandy once the girl was on her feet. Now that they stood together, Tabitha had passed her up and was inching closer to the ceiling. Her tightly spun hair was now falling down and getting longer by the minute.

"I don't think so," she said.

"Look down."

Both women stared at their growing, sensitive feet on the thin carpet. "Okay?"

"It's said that in nature, you can only truly absorb the Earth's energy through your feet."

Both women became even hairier, their arms and legs lined with coarse, thick fur. The other women of the room yelped, having been too transfixed by their bushes to notice how their legs and arms had become covered.

"Look at my feet, and let's look at yours," she said, and turned her legs up so they could see the soles of her feet. They were rough—which came with being exclusively barefoot for the last year. The other girls by comparison had soft, well-maintained soles from constant pampering and shoes.

"They're so rough," said Tabitha. "I bet you can walk across anything."

"I can and I have," said Mandy. "That's the focus of grounding. To touch nature, to be one with it. We should do an experiment, eh?"

"But we're so high up," said Tabitha, looking out the window. Her eyebrows were becoming like soft caterpillars. And it was true—they *were* high up, overlooking the city. Storm clouds had gathered and it was soon to rain.

Mandy's own hair was coming in thick, her eyebrows bushy, her pubic hair like a small plant, and the stubble beneath her arms sticking out in haphazard clumps. If only the world could see her now.

"I have an idea."

***

In the middle conference room, while taking in the aromatic wonders of the Inner Beast incense, the change was happening all at once. True, it took longer to begin, as the good stuff wasn't even until halfway down the stick so that everyone could become acclimated and relaxed before they started to grow and sprout fur. But the tingling feet . . . that was always right away.

Angelica, who'd been the most uptight of all three Howling Sisters in the beginning, was the first to let loose. She undressed, propped her tingling feet up on the table for all the women to see, and then struck up an incense reed and let it burn right by her nostrils. The other women did the same thing, and just when the other two rooms had started to change—growing first or hair first—the incense room was just starting to mellow out.

"I think Kaitlyn should've come to this room," said Carol, a lady representing a clothing company called *New Girl*.

"Why's that?" asked Angelica.

"Because she'd love this hippy dippy crap. It's not for me."

"Is that so? Well take another whiff, ma'am," said Angelica, then leaned forward and waved the burning stick in her face.

Carol looked a little agitated, perhaps even a little perplexed, but soon after Angelina finished her final presentation—the big push to buy—the effects of the Wild Woman crop began to take over. And when it hit, it was like a flurry of activity.

"I wasn't into this 'hippy dippy crap' either," said Angelica. "But the stuff in this incense changed all that.

And I'm glad it did. I would never want to go back to the way things were before. So stifling."

Carol listened intently to her words and then began to grow in her seat, the clothes becoming cumbersome until she leaned back and shredded her top. She let out a tiny moan, then quickly looked around to verify if anyone had seen. Slowly, she was losing the battle of her inhibitions, and like Mandy and Christina, Angelica loved to watch it happen. Carol threw her feet up on the table, the toes poking through the pantyhose until they were shredded and snapped against the pads of her feet.

"They're so . . . tingly," she said, and when she leaned up to rub them, the chair snapped from its wheels and fell over. She lay in the floor laughing, along with everyone else. The whole room was going through a similar metamorphosis—Angelica included.

They were growing, legs and feet stretching out. Hair was starting to appear in large wads beneath their arms. Several of the girls had already gotten to their final heights of twelve feet tall, and since they were naked, the swell of hair between their legs was both quick and magical. Angelica loved watching that part, almost as much as watching the girls fondle themselves while it was happening. Carol's fingers reached into her own pussy, past the mat of newly grown hair, and started to play.

The hair on Angelica's head had just started to lengthen when she stood up, nearly bumping her head, and heard a commotion from out in the hallway. She rushed to the doorway, stepping over girls who were comparing feet, pleasuring themselves, or still going through the final phases of the metamorphosis, and looked out. When she saw several large shapes zip by, she smiled and turned back to the room, just as lightning flashed through the windows.

"Hey girls! Field trip!"

***

Kaitlyn didn't think she could become aroused anymore, but once the growing hair seemed to subside, a new adventure began. The tingle in her feet and lady parts never went away—but in fact intensified. It was true, just as she'd uttered it—she was growing. Not just her hair, which could get no longer—it was cascading down to her waist, and was in thick tufts beneath her arms and between her legs. But now, her whole body was shooting up—feet getting longer and thicker, breasts becoming fuller, ass more rounded. The lotion was a miracle product, and she wanted to buy every last drop of it. Hopefully once she told Carol all about it, her uptight boss would concur.

The other women in the room were likewise covered in fur. If they had curly locks before, they looked as though they had long, wavy houseplants atop their heads. If they had straight hair before, it was now like silk hanging down to their asses. And to see that hair multiply was nothing short of amazing—Kaitlyn was one of the first to grow, so she was able to watch from her 'perch' at nearly twelve feet tall and see the rest shoot up, her eye on bushes the whole time.

Her own fingers had already taken the plunge more than once, and she couldn't understand why she was feeling so . . . free. It couldn't have been the weed in the products—she'd smoked enough of that during college and it never phased her in such a way. It was almost as if the Howling Sisters had some sort of giantess-making-hair-growing magic.

Just as a storm began to form outside, she heard several people lumber by in the hallway—clearly they were of the giant variety because their weight and momentum resembled a train on the other side of the thin partition. Christina, now a nine-foot tall beauty with hair everywhere, stepped up to the window and pinched the blinds so she could see out into the hallway. A smile formed on her lips and she turned back to address the room.

"Okay, girls, we're going to play in the rain!"

It sounded so weird, so alien to Kaitlyn but for some reason she was totally onboard. Christina held open the door and the congregation of women filed out, joining another larger group of similar women. Kaitlyn would never forget what she saw in the hallway for as long as she lived.

There were around a hundred girls—all naked, or nearly naked. But each were giant-sized, some as little as nine feet tall, some as big as twelve feet, their heads brushing the ceiling and dodging the low-hanging fluorescent lights as they ran. Each of them was covered in hair—from their arms and legs, down to their armpits and bushes. In some places the hallway was so narrow, and the women so large, that they couldn't help but press against one another.

Halfway down the steps (for none of them could fit in the elevator) Kaitlyn ran into Carol—her uptight boss who was now flaunting her large tits and hairy bush. She looked just as free as the rest of them, and she offered Kaitlyn a smile as they rounded the steps and headed down and out of the building. When she looked at everyone else, Kaitlyn finally felt as if she fit in, and her angst at being here started to unravel. Outside, there was a movement— and she was happy to be a part of it.

***

"Never thought I'd see our handywork in such a way," said Mandy, now a hair-covered goliath. There was a news chopper heading over, but that wasn't surprising, nor would it be the last. The other two girls from the Howling Sisters came up beside her and looked across the crowd. Someone had started playing music and it was getting the girls worked up.

The rain was pelting down on them—a little cold for this time of the year, but a pleasant surprise after they'd been in the stifling conference rooms, the heat of arousal pumping up the temperature. Before them lay a crowd of almost a hundred women, all scaled up to nearly double their original size, and each one covered in so much hair that the plaza where they all danced had taken on a very earthy smell. The grass was sodden, and as Mandy stepped down in it, she could feel the mud squeeze between her toes. She looked back across the field where the women were trodding, and there was a circus of prints—all massive and deep—where stepped a hundred girls.

"C'mon girls, let's join the party." She ran into the crowd, slipping between several large, hairy bodies, and started to dance. Angelica and Christina weren't far behind, mingling and caressing bodies as they squeezed by. The tingles in Mandy's feet didn't go away, but, as she'd said before, the grounding made her feel positively electrified, as if she were connected to the Earth and all the women in the plaza.

Traffic had started to slow down, to gawk, to snap pictures. None of them cared. Perhaps their careers were on the line after such a stunt, but every woman present had lowered inhibitions. Mandy could see going into business with several of them, for after all—if The Howling Sisters were to become a household name, they needed partners.

Mandy found her way through the crowd again, coming upon Tabitha who was shaking her ass with the best of them. Her long, stringy hair was soaked and matted to her head. Her pubic hair was similarly pressed. She looked at Mandy and grinned, like a kid who just stole a cookie from the jar. Or perhaps just an uptight woman who'd learned to finally let go.

"This stuff is amazing," she said, balling her hands into fists and squeezing them. Water beaded off her knuckles.

"Do we have your support?" asked Mandy. "LadyWyk is quite the powerhouse."

"Sweetheart," said Tabitha, reaching in and pulling Mandy close by the neck. She put a long, wet and sloppy kiss on her lips. "If my higher-ups could see all this, they'd throw every penny they have at you!"

"I don't think that'll be a problem," said Christina by Mandy's ear. She turned and hooked her thumb up to the sky, where three helicopters hovered, watching the giant-sized semi-orgy take shape.

Mandy just grinned, blew a kiss, and waved.

A little while later after the gawkers seemed to no longer care, the Wild Woman crop was wearing off and the women were shrinking back and losing their hair. Now, they were plain and ordinary, although very naked. Mandy had come prepared, and while the women were in the midst of their transformation, she'd brought her van around to the plaza and opened the side door. The Howling Sisters doled out baggy shorts, tee shirts (with the company logo on them) and a pair of cheap flip flops. The women collected their tattered clothes and were offered samples of the Wild Woman crop to take home. Then, the girls all dressed and stood around, as if not knowing what to do, and then they each began going their separate ways.

"Well would you look at that," said Christina pointing to the throng of women who were moving off.

"What is it?" Mandy asked, not understanding at first, but then she did.

Each of the women were walking off, dressed, but carrying their flip flops in their hands.

"They're choosing to be barefoot," said Angelica.

Mandy nodded. "Well it seems we made an impact."

***

One year later . . .

The Howling Sisters had become a corporate conglomerate. After their stunt made its way across the world, starting with social media and ending up on national news, everyone was curious about the group of giant, hairy, free-spirited women. Mandy, along with her co-CEOs, had bought up nearly every rival and companies like *LadyWyk* and *New Girl* carried a vast assortment of their products.

But a company could never be too big.

Almost a year to the day, Mandy was overseeing another conference, this one far out in the country, but able to draw enough people to fill a five-hundred seat auditorium. Both Christina and Angelica were on other projects—both overseas, so she handled this one on her own, alongside a new company upstart named Kaitlyn Danvers. The girl had taken like a fish to water with the products, and could sell just about anything. As they mounted the stage in front of so many people—enough people in fact, that they had to wear headset connected to the sound system—both women bowed and got started.

"You're all here because you wanna get big!" said Mandy to thunderous applause.

"And you wanna get hairy!" added Kaitlyn, to just as much fanfare.

"Well now is your chance to do both. We want to sell you our products, but we also want you to experience them. That's precisely what you're gonna do today!"

And then, men in towers began lobbing what appeared to be grenades into the field of women. Some were startled, but Kaitlyn assured them it was okay. "Don't panic, ladies, it's all part of the show."

After that, the canisters burst open and a greenish fog began to fill the air. The women crowding around knew what it contained, and rather than run off, they drew closer. Instantly the effects were apparent, a low ripple of moans ran through the crowd, followed by the groan of clothes and shoes.

"Ready to have some fun?" asked Kaitlyn after she pulled off the headset.

"Damn straight I am." Mandy joined her in the crowd, disappearing inside the green mist, feeling her body starting to change. . .

Jack's New Life

The Follow-Up Story to Short One No More

Amber was a little worried that Beth would take things too far with Jack. Having the matter reducer in hand gave someone far too much power. And coupled with years of abuse from a gargantuan man, it would be quite easy to abuse that power. And while Amber was mostly onboard with anything Beth wanted to do, she didn't like the idea of the girl botching her plans by harming Jack. If she did something that got the authorities involved, it could scrap the whole project—there'd be no more shrinking and growing for anyone.

Currently, she was standing on Beth's doorstep. It had been two days since she'd last seen her coworker—and the abusive husband—and she wondered how well the brute had fared. However, 'brute' was probably not the right word to describe him now. Jack had been nearly seven-foot-tall before Beth brought home the MA—the Matter Arranger. Jack had been a six-inch man when Amber last left.

The door swung open and she saw his luck hadn't improved much. He looked up at her—from a height of only three feet tall. He was dressed in normal clothes, as Beth had no doubt shrunken them down to fit him. His eyes were rimmed in red, as if he hadn't been sleeping well. But that was probably the case, as Beth surely wasn't being gentle with him. Amber had never seen someone look so defeated. And she'd never seen someone who once looked so large and muscular now look so tiny and helpless.

"Hello, little guy. Is the big lady of the house here?"

He just stepped aside and held the door open, his little shoulders hunching and his eyes flinching when heavy footfalls sounded on the tile behind him. A giant set of legs approached and stood just behind him, and his head dropped as though he was too afraid to make a movement.

Amber couldn't see all of Beth because she was scaled up to be around twelve feet tall, and the giantess had to stoop to make eye contact.

"Hey girl, how's it going?" the big lady asked. She was absolutely gorgeous. She'd been so small her whole life, barely above four feet tall, but now her breasts were pushing out through the doorway, her nipples erect beneath a tight-fitting shirt. When she stood up and moved aside, her ass filled the whole kitchen, so large and bulbous.

"Fine," said Amber. "Just thought I'd come by to check on things."

"Well come on in!" she said. "Little man was about to get started on me. But I guess he can get started on you, too."

"Sounds nice," said Amber, feeling a tingle run down her body. She'd played with the tiny man before, and he was quite adept at pleasing a woman much larger than himself.

"Can I get you tea?" asked Beth. And before Amber could even say yes or no, she quickly turned to Jack and said, "Our guest is thirsty! Put on a pot of tea now."

"Okay," he said, flatly.

"Okay?"

"Yes, ma'am," he corrected.

"Much better." She smiled at Amber before turning and ducking through the doorway to head into the living room. Her massive ass and breasts were shaking and wobbling with each step she took.

The two women sat and talked for a moment while Jack fixed their tea.

"So I think Nick really wants in on the action," said Amber. "He's hinted around at it. I want to shrink him and make him my plaything."

"Playthings are great," said Beth, looking back into the kitchen where the little man was on a stool and pouring hot water with wobbly hands. "I adore mine."

"But that's not what I mean," said Amber. "I want to be gentle with mine. I also want to be small with him. Ride that giant cock of his. I'm thinking of asking if he's game."

"You know he would be. The guy is crazy about you. And who wouldn't wanna fuck a giantess?"

"This is true, big lady. Maybe I'll keep him normal sized and get big myself."

"Now you're talking!" said Beth.

Just then, Jack walked into the room carrying a platter with two steaming cups of lavender tea. He placed them on the coffee table and then left, entering the kitchen and cleaning up. Amber could see him in there on his hands and knees, scrubbing the floor near the stove, and couldn't help but giggle over how the big man had become so much less. Never had he ever lifted a finger to help his wife around the house. Perhaps Beth wasn't mistreating him at all—in fact, he was only getting what he deserved.

"I'm gonna play with him. Feel free to watch or join in." And then, as Beth was sliding out of her pants, she said, "Little fucker! Get in here!"

Amber could see his silhouette in the kitchen stand up and seem to sigh. By the time he rounded the corner, he was completely naked. He would've looked like a child if not for the massive amount of muscles and the tattoos on his chest and legs. Beth completely disrobed, throwing her oversized clothes in the corner basket and then reclining back on the sofa. She put one leg up on the back and one in the floor, then spread them, pointing to her womanhood.

"Get to work, little guy."

He gave one embarrassed look to Amber and then dutifully got busy. He climbed atop the sofa between the giantess's legs and then leaned down, kissing her thighs first and then working up toward her sweet spot. Beth had one hand tweaking a nipple and one in her hair, tousling it from side to side. Her mouth fell open and it didn't take long for a few moans to escape.

Jack's licking and sucking became more audible, as the giantess was growing wetter with each pass of his tongue. His little hands were up on her stomach, rubbing gently, and Amber could see the goosebumps breaking out along her skin. He became forceful, tiny yet firm muscles clenching with each movement. Beth brought her legs down and wrapped them around his tiny body, to which the small man almost fell.

But the more Amber watched, the more aroused she became, and fingering herself wouldn't hit the spot. No, she needed to join in for sure . . .

Already she'd begun the task of unzipping her jeans and kicking off her flats. When they clattered to the floor, an ever-nervous Jack flinched and looked up, his chin dribbling with Beth's juices. The giantess quickly put him back on task, pushing his face down between her legs. She continued to moan, to writhe on a sofa that was too large for her, and thus was buckling dangerously in the middle.

When she peeked out of the corner of her eye and saw Amber now completely stripped down, hand working her clit, she lifted the tiny man up by the neck and redirected him off the sofa. He stood, locked in her grip, and waited. She pushed him toward Amber, who caught him and shoved him down by throwing her legs up on his shoulders. The tiny man went to his knees, a tiny cry escaping his lips from the hard landing. But he dutifully went to work, pleasing another pussy, albeit a much smaller one.

Jack was visibly tiring, and when his movements started to slow down, Beth rotated on the sofa and put a rather large foot directly on his back, coaxing him to pick up the pace. He did as she wordlessly commanded, his arms massaging Amber's inner thighs, his tongue making the trip back and forth along her slit. It was too small to go that deep, but it still felt good. Her thoughts continued to drift to Nick and his giant cock . . .

"Is my little man boring you?" asked Beth.

"What?" Amber asked, feeling her body relax. Jack's head was still bobbing up and down.

"You look like you were drifting off to sleep there for a minute. Want me to supersize you?" She held up the MA and programmed something into it.

"Sure!" said Amber, straightening.

Beth blasted her in the chest and the effects were almost immediate. The tiny man beneath her seemed to get even tinier as she grew, but mostly because her breasts had shot out, ballooning up in the most unnatural way. The little guy was lost beneath them. Her ass also got wider, propping her up on a cushion she could take wherever she chose. Her legs moved out, toes curling along the edges of Beth's sofa. Amber's head rose up as the seat bowed down. And then, she brought a hand to the tiny man's head, now feeling like an apple. She'd grown to match Beth—around twelve-feet tall.

Now, Jack was small enough to really abuse, so she squeezed his head, just hard enough to take control, and moved him as she wished. She brought her back down hard on the sofa so she could push out her hips, and then she did a little dance up and down, running his face along her slit, pushing his lips and nose into her. She was soaking wet, and the little man made a gurgle. Beth just watched and laughed, but her foot was still on his back, keeping him from escaping. And just when Amber hit her first and largest orgasm, she brought her thighs in hard, gripped his tiny head between them, and rode it out for as long as she could. When it was over, she was squirting all over his face, and the tiny many wound down to a hunched sob, and then collapsed onto the carpet.

Both girls looked down at him and laughed, but it was Amber who used a large foot to flip him over on his back. He looked as if he'd been swimming.

"You been running Jack like this the whole time?" Amber asked.

Beth grinned. She was rolling him around with the heel of her foot, his tiny body almost weightless. "Of course. I give him breaks because if I don't, he gets sloppy. Don't ya, boy?" She kicked him in the ribs, just hard enough to make him sit up, cough, and nod.

"I bet this must suck, huh dude?" Amber said. "Being seven feet tall. Kicking the shit out of your girl. I guess if you wanted to play those games you needed a stupid girl. You can't do that to a genius. Didn't you know your girl is smart? If you'd have had a conversation with her instead of hitting her, you might've."

He didn't say anything, only looked up at them in shame. He wasn't sorry for what he'd done, only sorry that things had turned out in such a way. Amber put her large foot right between his legs, her sole touching his tiny, laughable cock. "I think you should give me a foot rub," she said. "And after that maybe a pedi. My toes are looking kinda rough lately."

"Nah, fuck that," said Beth, pulling out the MA and typing in data sets. Jack stood up and whirled around, his face already breaking down. He'd learned to recognize the sound of the device, and it brought fresh waves of panic from him every time Beth picked it up.

"More fun?" asked Amber.

"You betcha," said Beth. "He knows that our game doesn't end with him this size. No, no, little Jack. The game is done when you're a pussy plug." She zapped him right in the chest.

He backed up, as if propelled by the force of the raygun. Amber put her hands on his shoulders only to feel them quickly slipping away, moving down, down, down toward the carpet. He didn't try to run. Jack only hung his head in shame and perhaps fear because he knew what was coming next.

"I have it written down," said Beth, holding up an index card she'd pried from the coffee table. "The perfect size for him when I'm twelve feet tall. We've had time to experiment and let me tell ya, sister—this is the best height for a little pussy pleaser."

"I hope I get to try him out."

"I'll give you first dibs. Have at him," she said. By now, Jack had dwindled away to nearly nothing. In truth, he was probably a foot or so tall, but that size was negligible when the women themselves were twelve feet in height.

Amber held out her foot, carrying him back toward the middle of the floor by her toes. She picked him up which was a precarious balance as he struggled to land atop her foot. And then, she held it straight and said, "Walk to your worksite."

He just nodded, but her leg was too unstable to walk cleanly across, so he got down on his knees and gripped it between his legs and his arms. This made the girls laugh hysterically, but he did make it, and when he was in her lap, she pushed him inside her pussy, head first. He struggled, but the moment he straightened his back and legs, she shoved him hard, and he disappeared completely. Amber held a hand over her lips in case he decided to leave before she allowed it.

"Oh, fuck! You're right. This is a good size indeed!" Her eyes were rolling into the back of her head.

The women passed the next hour in this way, handing him off to the other for deep sea exploration. When one came, the other helped pull him out and then their roles reversed. By the time it was over, they'd soaked the living room, and the little man seemed to be hanging on for life. His body was starting to shrivel after being submerged in juices for so long.

They were about to go another round, but then the doorbell rang.

"Who could that be?" asked Amber, looking back and trying to see through the tiny window next to the door.

Beth had pulled up her phone, and that's when Amber remembered that her friend had one of those wireless doorbell cameras, and she was currently checking the app to see the live feed. Instantly, her face warmed and she smiled. She turned her phone around so that Amber could see.

Standing on her doorstep, making uncomfortable eye-contact with the camera, was Nick. He was wearing his casual clothes—tee shirt, jeans, and chucks. She didn't understand why he'd come over to Beth's, but it was probably to see Amber. He'd no doubt driven by her house, saw the car missing, and came here. But what did that mean, exactly?

"Go answer the door," said Beth.

"Shrink me back!" she said.

"Nope. And no clothes either. I dare ya, girl. Just go answer it. I guarantee this will cut through a lot of the red tape. It'll speed things up."

"You're crazy!" said Amber. "He'll run away."

"No, girl. You don't get that guy. He'll run face first into that pussy."

That made Amber's cheeks turn red, but it also made her want to find out. She pulled her hair back, nevermind the fact that her own cum was dribbling down her thigh. She stood up, head nearly brushing the ceiling, and stormed toward the door. Nick was visibly shaken on the front porch—she could see this through the tiny, half-moon window at the top of the door. He'd no doubt heard the footsteps coming toward him.

She was about to rock his world.

***

He didn't know what the noise was on the other side of the door although he should've been able to guess it. Both he and Amber had stormed around the lab in their mega-sized shoes, so the reverberations of a giant foot shouldn't have been odd. But when the door opened, he wasn't prepared for what he saw. All that he knew was that he couldn't see all of it.

Currently there was a giant set of feet, legs, and pussy on the other side of the doorframe. He'd had enough experience with the MA so that he wasn't thrown off by the appearance of a giant person, although a fully naked one was something different. And as much as he'd studied Amber, as much as he'd lusted after her, he had no question whose face was at the top of this gorgeous body.

She sank down on her knees, her enormous breasts filling the doorway from left to right. He couldn't pull his eyes from her erect nipples. They were pointing at him, coaxing him inside Beth's house, as if to say *come play with us*. He managed to bring his eyes back to hers, which were beaming at the sight of him.

"Hey, sexy," she said. It was a word she'd never used to describe him but he liked it, nonetheless.

He didn't have much of a reply, other than a "hey" back.

"What are you doing here?" she asked, turning her head to the side, genuinely curious.

"I . . . uh. . . came by your house to see if you were home. I was out for a drive, ya know? And I didn't see your car so I thought I'd come here and . . ." His voice trailed away as he turned to hook his thumb back toward her vehicle, the little two-door sedan, sitting in Beth's driveway.

"Uh huh. And what did you need?" she asked. She'd sat down, rather than invite him in. He knew why— she'd rather see him get worked up and do his best to avoid staring.

"Uh, well." He instinctively put a hand over his pocket, but that was the only tell she needed. Her eyes lit up and she lashed out, fingers digging into his jeans. Before he even realized what she was doing, she had it out, pinched between her thumb and forefinger.

"Did you plan to play with me?" she asked, holding up the prototype MA.

He looked away, embarrassed, and ran a hand across his bald head as always.

"It's okay, Nick. Tell me. I really wanna know." And then, she held out her hands, arms disappearing on the other side of the doorway, and shook her breasts. They wiggled back and forth and then came to an abrupt rest. "I don't think we have many secrets. Fess up."

"Well . . . I wanted . . . to fuck you."

"And?"

"I wanted you to be big and then I wanted to get big with you."

"Oh yeah?"

"Yeah."

"And what if I said yes?"

He looked back, face lighting up. "Then I'd be stoked."

"I would totally be up for it," she said, voice trailing and eyes looking off. "But I have a condition."

"Name it," he said.

"You gotta fuck Beth too."

He paused for a moment, gathering himself. This was something he wasn't expecting.

"Beth is married."

"Beth is going through something. Suffice it to say, she's single and ready to mingle."

"What about Jack?" Nick asked. "I don't want trouble. That dude could beat the shit out of me so bad that I wouldn't be able to walk again."

At this, Amber threw her head back and laughed.

"What?" he asked.

"That's the beauty of our situation, Nick. You're gonna fuck me. And you're gonna fuck Beth. And Jack is gonna watch and do nothing about it."

He just stared at her, waiting for her to explain the rest of it. "You're going to have to give me a little more than that."

"How about I just show you?" she said, then she got up, bracing herself on the wall above the doorway and moved back. "Come on in."

His first thought upon entering the house was that he wanted to match her size—that he wanted to fuck her—and Beth, and knew he was probably inadequate at his current height. And when he rounded the corner and entered the living room, he realized this was exactly the case. Beth was sitting in the floor, her body swelled to the same size as Amber's—both sets of breasts the largest he'd ever seen. On the coffee table, pushed in the corner, lay a tiny man sleeping. It was Jack, and he was soaking wet—it didn't take a genius to realize what had happened to him.

"Is he okay?" asked Nick, his voice barely above a whisper.

"He's fine," said Beth. "We just made him earn his keep, is all. How goes it, short stuff?" She brought her hand down and patted Nick's head.

"Thought I'd come say hi," he said, smiling gently. "I must say, you girls look pretty amazing." He took it upon himself to stroke Amber's leg, who had just seated herself on the sofa. She looked down at him and grinned.

"Oh yeah?" said Beth. "You want in on this action?" She spread her legs so there was no question at all of what she meant.

"Definitely," he said, and without an ounce of shyness, he stripped down to nothing, his massive cock swinging back and forth. The girls looked at it with a mix of arousal and curiosity—as if they wondered whether or not it would currently fill them up. "Alright, girls. Zap me up."

Both of them laughed hysterically, and it was enough to stir the tiny man from his sleep. He looked up, his face glowering, and then he turned over and fell back asleep, powerless.

"What?" asked Nick, giving his dick a gentle stroke.

"You have to earn your size," said Amber. She sat up straight and spread her legs, fingers inching down her stomach to massage her clit. "So come earn it."

He grinned and dropped to his knees between Amber's legs. Her thighs were breaking out in goosebumps before he even made it close to her sweet spot, so he licked along her flesh and by the time he made it to her pussy, she was already dripping. It all felt weird in his mouth—her lips were unusually long, her clit unusually bulbous. None of it was a bad thing, but being a normal-sized man trying to please a double-sized pussy was rather unique. Still, he was up for the challenge, and unlike Jack, he was quite willing to get the job done.

"Looks like Nick has some skills," said Beth across the room. "Or maybe he's just wanted that pussy for so long."

"Can it be both?" he said through slurps.

He continued to work Amber long enough for the girl's legs to shake and quiver and drown them both, then he walked across on his knees so he could do the same for Beth. Her pussy was only slightly smaller, but on a twelve-foot tall woman, that was hardly relative. He worked her just as well, but the orgasm was a little harder to pull out of her. By the time he was ready to try his dick, he'd gotten both women off several times.

Amber was the first he attempted to fuck. The giantess slid into the floor and leaned back on the sofa's cushion so Nick could line himself up properly. And although he had a giant dick, it hardly made waves for a twelve-foot woman. There was very little resistance, and the only thing that seemed to drive her wild was the way he played with her clit on each pass. Her love tunnel was just too big to accept him, but he thought he'd give Beth a try, just to be sure.

Her sudden giggles told him that it wasn't working for her, either. He looked up at her face, and there was no pleasure or pain, just a giant pair of breasts heaving back and forth with each of his thrusts. She tried to pretend like it was getting the job done but he knew better. Instead, he climbed up her and popped one of her massive nipples into his mouth, his hands still trying to reach below and massage her clit.

"Little guy, this just isn't cutting it," she said, pulling him away. She lifted him by the arms and stood him in the center of the room, as if considering him.

"Have I earned my size yet?" he asked.

Beth flashed a look back to Amber and gave her a wink. "What do you think, girl?"

"He got me awfully wet. And seeing as how that cock isn't much use right now, I say zap his ass."

Nick just stroked his dick, waiting. Beth pulled out the MA, made an adjustment on the touchscreen, then zapped the tiny man.

He gave a shudder, as he always did when the ray's magic worked through him, and then he was shooting up, his head coming within an inch of the ceiling. The girls couldn't pull their eyes away from his massive cock as it elongated, growing taller and thicker. Now, it looked like it could do a little damage, and they were both quite willing to give it a try.

"Wait," said Beth, before he dropped to his knees and positioned himself in front of her. "I want to wake the little fucker. He needs to watch this." She brought a hand down hard against the coffee table, and Jack violently awoke, assessing his surroundings and finally settling on the giant man in his house. It filled the tiny guy with fury, but there was nothing to be done about it.

"What's up, little guy?" said Nick. "Your lady called me over because she said you couldn't handle her. I can see why. Hold up that little dick."

When he didn't move, Beth slammed her fist on the coffee table and said, "He told you to hold up your dick!"

Jack reluctantly did as they asked, then turned away. Nick got down on his knees and held up his own massive cock, and the comparison was extreme. His dick was bigger than the tiny man's whole body, so seeing Jack holding that tiny sliver of meat between his fingers was quite comical. Nick slammed his cock down on the table, shaking it and sending the tiny man to his knees. Jack stood up, his eyes filled with venom, but Nick found it rather humorous.

"I gotta fuck these ladies now, dude," said Nick. "Beth said you couldn't satisfy her even at normal size. Guess you're shit out of luck now, huh?" That brought a round of laughter from both women, and made the little man on the coffee table fume even more.

Nick turned around and thrust his dick right into Beth's waiting pussy. The giantess made a ragged moan and leaned into him, scraping her nails along his back. She was looking over his shoulder, to the tiny man who could only watch as some guy fucked his wife. She was licking her lips and grinning, and despite Jack being seven-foot-tall once upon a time, he still couldn't fuck her the way Nick was right now.

It didn't take long to bring her to an orgasm, his cock filling her up so completely that it was borderline painful. If she didn't relax, he would probably do some real damage to her pussy. Still, she met the challenge, and by the time she'd gotten off three times, they'd wrecked the living room. Amber could only watch.

"Don't get him off," she said to Beth when Nick's stomach muscles began to quiver. "I want a turn."

He pulled out his cock, a sopping, wet mess, and stuck it into his work crush. Amber lay back, her head against the sofa, legs up over his shoulder. They were all watching the tiny man who was watching them just as intently. No matter what, he seemed unable to pull his eyes away from the massive trio fucking in his living room.

Beth decided to grow Jack back a little while Nick was busy with Amber. He looked over his shoulder and watched as the tiny man tried to please his wife, but it just wasn't happening.

Again, Nick was about to shoot his load, but Beth stopped him, her arms wrapping around his stomach and pulling him free of the other woman. She kissed along his neck for a moment and then whispered into his ear an idea. He was a little on the fence about it at first, but when he saw the groveling, tiny man over on the sofa, he decided he was game.

"We're gonna try something, little Jack," said Beth. "Stand up straight for me. Now." He wasted no time doing as she asked, fearing the retribution that might come if she became angry.

She pulled out the MA, to which he began to nervously back up, but she'd already input the data and zapped him. He froze in place, knowing there was no use in trying to escape. This was the smallest he'd ever become—he quickly dwindled down, reaching around an inch in height. The world, and the three giants, probably looked incredibly scary to him. Beth leaned down and scooped him up. He was small enough to sit across her finger.

She dabbed him on the head of Nick's cock, the tiny man screaming, but lodged in place by pre-cum and the juices of two women. Then, Beth got on her back and waited, knowing this was going to be interesting.

Nick pushed his dick in, the little man leading the way, and started to fuck Beth as hard as he could, her massive breasts jiggling side to side. Amber came around the side and latched on to one, sucking a nipple while Nick continued to pound. He didn't know what was happening to the tiny man inside, but it probably wasn't good. He was probably out of air, and if he wasn't, he would be soon. Nick's entire body shuddered and then, in the final throes of orgasm, he shot his load inside Beth, most likely drowning the little man in his stick, hot goo.

***

Jack thought he was dead after that, but he slipped off to sleep, assuming he'd never wake again. But when he opened his eyes again, he found himself on a bed—and appeared to be normal-sized, although he couldn't place where he was. He sat up and threw off the covers and looked around. The room was rather sparse—only the bed and a dresser near the window. He peered through the curtains and could see buildings—skyscrapers that he couldn't place. He stood and walked over to the window, throwing it up so he could gaze out, but something was wrong . . . something looked off with the city.

And then the ground started to shake.

He nearly toppled to his knees just as a giant foot appeared outside the window. He scrambled away from it, but it didn't matter. The entire roof of the house came away, and staring down at him was a colossal Beth—she had to be a thousand feet tall, as the buildings outside only came up to her ankles. She reached down and pulled the tiny, struggling man out, and then put him in her palm.

"You didn't think we'd let you die, did you?" she asked, voice booming. "We still have plenty for you to do." As he sat there, he looked around, and he noticed that things were not as they seemed.

The city below was a miniature, hand-painted to look like the real thing. The house where he'd been sleeping—merely a dollhouse. Above him, the sun was nothing more than a heat lamp. It was all a ruse.

"I don't . . . understand," he said.

"I'll fill you in, silly. You're my pet now. This is your home. And I am the mayor this town. Call it whatever you want. Jackville for all I care. But this is how things are now. Do you understand?"

He was quiet.

She squeezed her hand around him, just enough to show him she meant business.

"Answer."

"I understand."

"Good," she said, then placed him back on the bed. "Now get some rest. Amber's coming over later and we need a little stress relief."

And before he could even protest—not that he would—she replaced the roof and stormed away, shaking his tiny room.

The Ottoman

Nick didn't have many friends he could count on quite the way he could count on Amber. They'd been inseparable for the last year and a half. Both loved to tell the story that they hated each other at first—it was somewhat true. College English had been where they met, sitting right across from each other in Mr. Krombie's class. Amber noticed Nick's muscles first, just like any girl would. Nick notice her large, voluminous ass, giant breasts and smock of red hair—like any guy would. But even though they were destined to be great friends, it didn't seem as if they were going to be anything else. That was okay with both of them, which Nick found surprising.

He always said he couldn't be just friends with a girl, there had to be some sort of physical contribution to the relationship. And Amber was such a beautiful person that it had been hard not to put hands on her. Nick was afraid she'd start looking at him like a brother, and one afternoon she even changed in front of him, showing him her giant breasts—she had beautiful, dark nipples. He wanted to touch them, but knew better. It would have ruined their relationship.

So that's how life had been for the two, up until the day they discussed their mutual fantasy. Both had a size fetish. Nick loved the idea of being smaller, shrinking down and playing with a giant-sized woman's body. And luckily, Amber's own fantasy complimented it quite well. She wanted to interact with a tiny man. This led to hours of discussion, and they were both pleasantly surprised when they discovered that each other had frequented the same message boards for many years without being wise to the other.

It was an interesting fantasy for them because they were both so tall. Each stood at a commanding six feet. Nick looked like a bouncer with his muscles and his slick, bald head. Amber like a model with her giant breasts and huge ass. Her red hair spilled down across her chest and only accentuated her curves.

"Tomorrow is Valentine's Day," said Nick as they sat across from each other, watching some silly sitcom of which he couldn't even remember the name. They were at her house, a nice little three-bedroom place on a very quiet street.

"Yep," she said, her voice falling a little.

"We never have anyone on that day," he said. "I mean, no significant other."

"You're my significant other," said Amber, smiling at him.

"You know what I mean. We're always single. I've had what? Two girlfriends in the last year? You had that one guy with the truck."

"Brent."

"Yeah, Brent. Anyway, don't you get tired of not having someone?"

She grinned and shrugged. "Not really. You're all I really need."

That brought a smile to his face and he nodded. "Yeah, you're all I need too."

They continued watching the show again. After Amber got up to make them popcorn, she sat back down next to him. He straightened up, not sure why she'd decided to change spots. Amber smelled so good—she always did, and he wasn't sure if it was perfume or lotion. She put her head on his shoulder, which wasn't odd whenever they watched a movie, but today would be much different.

"I have a question," she said. "And don't get offended by it."

"Okay?"

"Promise?"

He thought about it and answered. "Promise."

"Are you lonely? Or are you just . . . horny?"

The way she said it made his dick start to firm up. The timing couldn't be worse, because her hand slithered down his stomach and gripped it through the pants. Now, he was hard as a rock and he looked into her eyes with great wonder.

"What are you doing?" he asked.

She giggled, her face turning red. "You were taking too long to answer, so I decided to find out for myself." Amber gave him a few test jerks and then let go, returning her hand to his leg. Still, she looked at him.

"That wasn't an answer," he said, nodding down to his cock. "You just caught him off-guard."

"Oh, is that what happened?" she said, smiling seductively.

His face was turning red, his heartbeat elevating.

"I need to go," he said.

"What? Why? No, Nick, please don't go!" She took her hands off him and stood up. "I'm sorry, I just . . . I get the same way too."

"What do you mean?" he asked.

"Dude. My vibrator just doesn't cut it these days. I need . . . you know, the real thing?"
"Yeah. I know what you mean."

"I didn't mean to make things awkward," she said. "You're a good friend."

"So are you," he said. But it *was* awkward after that. They went back to the television show, but there was now a defined line between them. Amber was sitting up straight, her feet on the floor. Nick watched her large breasts heave up and down from the corner of his eye. He really wanted her, and if he played his cards right, he could probably have her.

When the show came to a close, she stood up and said, "I want to show you something."

"Oh yeah?" he said, looking up at her. Between him sitting down and her standing, it was hard to see her face over her breasts. Up close, the girl was rocking a serious pair of sweater puppies.

She moved to the corner and pulled out an ottoman that he'd never noticed when he came over. It didn't match the furniture in the living room, and it looked old, almost as old as Ottoman Empire itself. The covering was red and embroidered with little golden fringes hanging off the sides. It was about three feet across, and about two feet high, making it a rather large accessory to the living room set. Amber pushed it out into the center of the room, just by the coffee table.

Then, she stood on it.

"Stand up, I'm going to be your giantess for a little while."

He grinned and did as she asked, now coming up to her large breasts. With the help of the ottoman, she was around eight feet tall.

"Lovely," he said, and fought the urge to touch them. But then, he didn't have to grab at all. Amber laughed, and when she did, she turned to the side, forcing her breasts right into his face. She smacked him, hard enough to stagger him back a step, and he looked up at her in surprise.

"Sorry, Nick. The girls have a mind of their own!" She was still laughing, but so was he. It was incredibly arousing to touch her breasts, even if they were still inside her shirt.

He hovered his hand over them, but then dropped it, feeling his face turn red from embarrassment. "This is a nice fantasy," he said. "Thanks for breaking the ice."

She stared down at him, hands on hips and said, "This is just the beginning."

"How so?"

And then there was Amber's little sheepish grin, the one that she often gave when she had a juicy secret, or perhaps a little bit of gossip. It was like that one time when her neighbor was sneaking over a man whenever her husband left for work. Nick didn't think this smile reflected those similarities, but it was making him curious, nonetheless.

"I want you to close your eyes and turn around," she said.

He pursed his lips and narrowed his eyes, unsure of what was up her sleeve. At the very least he might get hit in the back of the head with her massive breasts, so he played along. Nick turned around and clamped his eyes shut.

"Are they really closed? Like really tight?" she asked, putting hands on his shoulders. Without him realizing it, she'd walked him back toward the sofa a couple of steps.

"They are."

"Promise?"

"Promise. What are you doing?" he asked.

"You'll see."

She made a sound, as if she were doing a jumping jack. Her fingers were holding his shoulders tightly, and although he couldn't understand why, it was as though they were moving across his shirt without lifting. Something about her had changed. Her weight shifted, and she nearly pulled him back but he steadied himself. Amber was laughing hysterically.

"Eyes still closed?" she asked. Her voice sounded slightly different, as if she had moved off center behind him.

"Yep."

"Okay. Don't freak out, but open them and turn around." Her hands disappeared from his shoulders. When he turned, it took all that was in him *not* to freak out.

Amber was directly in front of him, standing at much the same height as before, only now the ottoman was behind her, and her bare feet were flat on the floor.

Everything about her had scaled up—her clothes, her earrings, her makeup and nail polish. She had increased in size to become an eight-foot woman. But as she moved and her breasts swayed, he realized she wasn't exactly proportional. Her breasts and ass had grown considerably larger, and now it looked like she was carrying a pillow inside her shirt and down the back of her jeans.

"What the actual *fuck*?" he said, looking her up and down.

"What do you think, Short Stuff?" Her breasts were swaying right in front of his face, and now they were the largest pair he'd ever seen. All he could do was stare. "I'll take your silence to mean you like it."

"Um . . . give me a minute to process things."

"Process this!" she said, then slapped him in the face with her breast. It was so hard and so forceful that he staggered back, almost returning to sit on the sofa. She held it up, and it was like a basketball between her large fingers.

"Is this for real?" he asked, and it sounded stupid coming out of his mouth, for it had to be real. There was an actual mini-giantess standing right in front of him. His dick was throbbing in his pants.

"Of course it's real."

"How?"

"Nevermind that now, Small Fry," she said. "What I want you to do is turn around again and close your eyes, okay?"

It made his heart beat fast because he could connect the dots here—she was about to do her little parlor trick again.

"Okay," he said, this time with far less hesitation and skepticism. He closed his eyes and spun back around to face the sofa.

There was movement behind him as she shuffled around the room and then she seemed to jump up and land on the carpet with a heavy thud. After that, she did it again, only the second thud sounded so much louder, so much deeper. He could hear a zipper, the quiet rustling of cloth, and then she told him to turn around, but her voice was ethereal, like it was floating in the air above him. Nick had an idea what he would see when he opened his eyes, but it still couldn't prepare him for it.

He was staring right into a giant pussy—shaved and slicked with juices because she was already so turned on. Her thighs, like massive tree trunks, were quivering in front of him. It was all so much to take in, but Nick was a boob guy, so his eyes looked past her beautifully toned stomach and found them, or at least their underside. Amber was now standing at a whopping twelve-feet tall, and her breasts completely shielded her face. She pulled them aside and looked down at him and smiled, her head seeming too massive to be real. His best friend was now double his size. Nick ran a nervous hand across his bald head, a little intimidated to be in her presence.

His eyes drank her in, moving up and down her body, from her perfectly pedicured toes up to her red hair that was sticking to the ceiling by static electricity. Her calves were toned and pushing out like shotguns. But his eyes fell to her pussy, to her clit that was the size of a golf ball, and to her slit that was longer than his whole face.

"I know you want it," she said, her hand gracing her stomach, her fingernails tracing little lines on her flesh. "You've wanted it for a long time and so have I."

"That's probably very obvious," he said, licking his lips.

She gave herself a nice, long stretch, her fingers scraping the ceiling. Amber said, "Go on then, get to servicing me, little man!"

Nick didn't need to be told twice.

She stood very still as he leaned in, first kissing her lips, then running his tongue along them. Amber's whole body broke out in goosebumps and it was mesmerizing to watch them ripple through the surface along her thighs. He only gave this a moment of his time and quickly returned to work. Her hand fell atop his head, her weight probably more than she realized.

She was getting wet and getting hot. Her scent was driving him crazy, driving his face deeper. Shaky hands came up and stroked her thighs, eliciting a tiny yelp of surprise before settling down. Nick gave her soft kisses along her skin. Amber's breathing was increasing, and he could tell she was getting worked up. He always wondered how this particular act would play out in the real world versus his fantasy. He assumed in real life, his tiny tongue and small hands wouldn't be up to par when it came to pleasing a giantess. But if her soft, guttural sounds were any indication, he was certain she was enjoying it.

He took his hands and wrapped them around her thighs, but they hardly went very far. Her legs and ass were so massive now that it was like trying to cup a wall. Still, he dug his fingers gently into her flesh and pulled her toward him, and pulled himself deeper into her pussy. His whole face disappeared into her slit, still licking, sucking, and kissing. The harder he pushed his face, the more she moaned and the weaker she became. Currently, she was using her massive hand to steady herself against the wall, for her knees were shaking with arousal.

Nick stole a quick glance up to see her face, and remembered that he wouldn't be able to see it because of her breasts, especially with his face planted so deeply inside her. But by the way her boobs heaved in and out, the way her breaths became ragged, he knew that she was still having a good time.

And then there was the juices.

She was getting so wet now that it was running down her thighs and over his face. When she held her breath, he knew that there was an enormous orgasm coming. He backed away, but only a few inches, and then she was gushing across him. It was so forceful that it knocked his head back. Her warm juices were flowing across his whole face and dripping down his chin and soaking through his shirt. He pulled it off over his shoulders, but it was too late. It was as if he'd jumped into a swimming pool.

"Look at that bod," she said, and she knelt down to rub her hands across his chest. Her face was so massive, currently splotched red from her multiple orgasms. Each time she breathed out, her breasts pumped, and he thought her nipples looked like tiny balloons at the ends of her areolas. His hand reached out and took one between his fingers and thumb.

It didn't take long to harden up, turning to stone at his touch. She grinned and let him play with for a few minutes, then brought the other around so he could show it a little love also. She was incredibly turned on, as was evidenced by the way she kept moaning, kept using her fingers to massage her clit, and kept pushing her breasts toward his outstretched hands.

"You get a gold star for that pussy licking!" she said. "Shall we take this to the bedroom for round two? I won't fit on the bed—it actually won't even support my weight, but we can still have fun in there."

"Lead the way," he said. He couldn't help but notice how she already knew that her weight would crash the bed—sure, it was a given that she was far heavier now, but the way she said it told Nick that she'd been big like this before.

When she turned to head into the bedroom, she put her ass right in his face, forcing him to back up. Then, she got down on her knees and crawled away from him, bringing his arousal to an even higher level than he thought possible. The way it shook back and forth as she kneed her way through the doorway nearly made his heart skip a beat. She was so gorgeous, and he couldn't wait to see where this went next.

After she crawled into the bedroom, she got up on her knees and pushed the bed as far back into the corner as she could. Then, she turned around and sat on her ass with her legs bent, but spread, as if beckoning him on. The twinkle in her eye drove him wild—he wondered just how long she'd been doing this, and for how long was the option available to have this kind of fun.

"Don't worry about me," she said, already reading the hesitation in his eyes. "I'll be back to normal tomorrow. How about we make the most of it tonight?"

She reached out, snatched the waist of his jeans and pulled him closer. He quickly shed them, kicking his pants and shoes into the corner. She helped lift him up until he was precariously balancing himself on her knees, putting his now too-small dick right in her face. She leaned in and started to suck him. He kept his eyes trained straight down, watching her breasts bunch up against her legs as she bobbed her head back and forth.

He would blow his wad at any moment, but she was too smart to let that happen. So, she gave him one final, long tug, then lifted him back down. With her hands forcefully on his shoulders, she pushed him onto his knees. Nick assumed she wanted him to go back to licking, but when he started to move his face toward her waiting pussy, she shook her head.

"Try to fuck me," she said, spreading her legs and bringing one down on his shoulder, to which he almost pitched forward.

"Okay," he said, and moved toward her on his knees.

He lifted his dick and pushed it into her pussy, but there wasn't much *oomph* behind it. Before she realized he was penetrating, his entire eight inches was inside, and his stomach was resting against her pubic bone. She covered her mouth with a hand, stifling a giggle. He wasn't as emasculated as he thought he would be, but that was because he was half her size. No shame to be had.

Nick picked himself up by putting his palms on her stomach and lifting, his tiny dick going in and out. However, his stomach rubbed her clit, and with each pass she gave a little shake, and it was making her toes curl. Still, this wasn't the way she wanted to get off, so she said, "Slide on back down. That tongue is way better. No offense."

He obliged his giantess.

It only took a few minutes to get her off again, and now that they were on the floor, her juices were able to hit him even harder. Once he was finished, he climbed back up and started kissing her cheeks, neck, and breasts, as he'd wanted to do for so long now. Sex wouldn't work for him any more than it would for her, so she wrapped her lips around his cock and sucked him off, quickly and efficiently.

"How did you do this?" he asked, still kissing the space between her breasts. He could almost fit his whole body between them.

"That's my little secret," she said. "Just enjoy the steak, sweetheart. Don't ask me where the meat comes from."

"What?"

"Nothing," she said, laughing.

***

He ended up sleeping over that night, nestled within the crook of the giantess's arm. She'd fished them blankets out of the closet and made them a paddock right on the floor. And true to her word, the next morning he awoke to much less Amber—she'd shrunken back down to normal-size through the night. As he watched her sleep, he couldn't help but find her just as beautiful. Her body was still a work of art.

Nick tiptoed out of the room to use the bathroom. As he was sitting there, he began to ponder just how she'd become so large. It was obviously something she could control. But what was the catalyst? Did she secretly drink a potion? Zap herself with a grow gun? Or was it something more obvious than that?

He went into the kitchen and started a pot of coffee, and while he was sitting on the sofa waiting for its wonderful aroma to fill the house and wake his friend, he made a connection with the ottoman. When she first pretended to be a giantess, she had been standing on it, and the next thing Nick knew, she made it a reality. Was her growth tied to the ottoman somehow?

He remembered the thumps.

Yes! She'd made two of them, the second one much deeper than the first, as if her increase in size had been in stages. Amber had *jumped* off the ottoman, and when she landed, she grew a little. That had to be it!

As he began to smell the coffee, a naughty thought struck him. What if *he* jumped off it? Amber was back to her normal size. He could take a few leaps, scale up to twelve feet tall, then have his friend suck his gigantic cock. It sounded like a lot of fun, and as she'd clearly displayed, it wasn't permanent. Just the thought of it had his dick getting hard between his legs. Nick was going to do it.

He stood up on it, imagining himself growing to twelve feet tall. He was completely naked and he surveyed the room, seeing it much as she saw it the day before. And a moment before he jumped, he could've sworn that he felt some kind of invisible force pushing down on his shoulders. And when his feet landed on the carpet, he expected himself to be much taller, but that wasn't the case. In fact, things were looking much bigger.

Nick was now only three feet tall.

"What the fuck!" he said, looking at his surroundings. Everything was twice as big—the sofa, Amber's shoes in the corner, the umbrella stand by the door. It made him a little fearful, as if the magic contained in the ottoman had misfired. He was trying his best not to panic. Nick couldn't have been more than three feet tall.

Just then, the bedroom door yawned open and out walked Amber, still half asleep, rubbing her eyes. No doubt she'd been stirred by the coffee. He vaguely remembered her telling him that she sleepwalked, that it scared her so badly because one time she got up and turned on the stove without even realizing it.

"Nick . . . you in here?" And then she bumped into him, his face right back where it had spent so much time yesterday. She looked down, saw him fall back against the ottoman, and it fully energized her.

"What's happening, Amber?" he said, looking at his own hands. "This is bad, right?"

Her face said otherwise. She put a hand on her hip and looked down at him.

"Someone tried to get big, huh? It didn't quite work out, did it?"

"How the hell is this possible?" he asked. "Where did you get the ottoman?"

"It's been passed down in my family for generations. My grandmother had it in the attic for years because she was afraid of its power. Girls get bigger each time they jump off it, and boys get smaller. No one really knows where it came from, but after mom died, I brought it here."

"So your grandmother, she had it all those years?"

"Yep! And when I was about twenty years old, I was cleaning her house. I stepped up on the ottoman to clear away cobwebs. Imagine my surprise when I stepped back down."

"I can't imagine. I guess this is quite a coincidence, huh?"

"How so?" she asked. She'd moved away and sat down on the sofa, her giant, glistening pussy on full display.

"It's a coincidence that you have a size fetish and happened upon a way to make yourself bigger."

She laughed at this and shook her head. "It didn't happen in that order. I found the way and *then* developed the fantasy. After that day I grew in grandma's house, I decided to run a few internet searches, see if anyone had ever heard of such a thing. And to my surprise and relief, there were whole communities dedicated to getting off to this kind of thing. I just fell in love with it after a while."

"That's pretty awesome," said Nick.

"Yep. So guess what?"

"What?" he asked.

"It's Valentine's Day. And you don't have me a gift."

"Or do I?"

She gave him a devious little grin and wink of the eye, then pulled him closer.

"You're my gift, Short Stuff. And you're not leaving here until you please me."

"I am more than fine with that," he said.

They took a shower together, which was a lesson in compression. Her standup tub was a tight fit for one person, and definitely for one and a half people. Nick took a wash cloth and lathered it up, then got on his knees and cleaned her legs and feet. He loved the feeling of the hot water beading down on his back, and he loved looking up at his wet goddess, the water running in rivulets across her breasts. Little drops fell from her nipples.

She pressed her forearms to the shower wall, and pushed his tiny body against her, his face right at her pussy. Amber was moaning, biting her lip, resting her forehead against the wall. He couldn't tell what was her juices or what was the hot, steaming water, but both refreshed and energized him. Again, her whole body was breaking out in goosebumps and her thighs were shaking. He'd never had his face in someone's pussy so much—the last two days accounted for more action than he'd had in the last seven years.

They dried each other off in the bedroom which was more of a task for Nick than it was for her. He simply patted her down as best he could, and when he was finished she took a large beach towel and wrapped it completely around his body, fitting more like a sheet than anything else. And when they were dry they moved back into the living room where she sat down on the sofa and assumed her favorite position.

She put her bare feet up on his shoulders, nearly bringing him to the floor, but she quickly wrapped her hands under her thighs for support. Amber took all her weight off him and allowed him to come forward.

He buried his face in her pussy once again, licking her sweet spot until he started to taste her wetness. After he'd gotten her off a few more times, she sat up, pulling her pussy away from him, and then lifted him beneath the arms.

"Where are we going?" he asked.

She sat him down on the ottoman.

"Jump, little man."

He didn't know what she had in mind, but he trusted her. He took a step forward and jumped.

His feet didn't hit the ground because she'd caught him, but now he was about half the size he was before— probably no more than eighteen inches tall. The room, and Amber, looked simply massive, and he didn't know what he could possibly do for her at this size. But then again, he wasn't staying eighteen inches. This was simply a transitory size. The real fun would come soon enough.

Amber placed him back on the ottoman.

"Seriously?" he said. Although he couldn't back out if he wanted. There was only one way for such a small man to leave this perch.

"Yep. Do it."

He closed his eyes and jumped. Again, he didn't hit the floor, for the floor would be too far a leap for such a small man. He opened his eyes and looked into the giant face of his best friend. She was simply massive. If he had to guess, he figured he was around six inches tall.

"Perfect," she said. "I've never done this before, but it should be fun."

"Done what?" he asked, but he already knew.

She moved back to the sofa and spread her legs, then deposited the tiny man right in front of her pussy. "You should know what. This is our fantasy, after all. You up for the task?"

"Yes ma'am," he said, and used his hands to part her lips. She brought down fingers to help and the trip inside was much easier.

He pushed past her muscles into her dark, wet love tunnel. He'd had his face and mouth all over this part of her and now it was simply the icing on the cake for his whole body to end up here. She was so hot and he worried about her muscles closing in on him, but she was vigilant in keeping him safe. He didn't have to move much for her to start squirting juices across him.

And when she finally did have her biggest orgasm, Nick brought his arms to the sides and kept his legs straight, making his body as aerodynamic as possible. She expelled him where he landed in a puddle between her legs. The massive woman before him was heaving, sucking in air like a beached fish. Her breasts were obscuring her face—but only until she brought him up and placed him between them.

"That was a ride!" he said.

"Yeah?"

"Hell yeah!"

She said, "Best. Valentine's. Day. Ever!"

The Writing on the Wall

Stephanie hadn't been back to her hometown in over six years but after her mom passed away, it was up to her to get all affairs in order. She was an only child, twenty-three years old and now in charge of her parents' estate. Luckily her mom had an insurance policy, and one on her dad, too, although that one had started to dry up years ago. The only thing left on Steph's agenda was to meet with the listing agent and sell the house. It would probably stay on the market for years but that was okay with her. She'd pay the taxes on it each year and let it rot. After this one, last nostalgic walk down memory lane, she would never return to her hometown again.

She came in a day early to see what sort of shape the house was in before letting another human inside it. Plus, although she wouldn't admit it to herself, she wanted to see how things had changed. Currently, she lived half a country away, and she'd opted to drive the whole way back. It was almost an eight-hour drive and as she was pulling through the underpass that would lead to her town, an incredible sense of nostalgia washed over her.

It looked exactly the same as before. The pizza place, the coffee shop, the laundromat and even the bowling alley were all still there. Sure, they had a facelift after so many years, but the businesses were intact. That brought a smile to her face, something she wasn't really expecting. But nothing could prepare herself for coming back to the house where she'd grown up.

If the town seemed unchanged, it was nothing compared to the two-story house in front of her. Even the siding was the same, the window treatments, the woodwork around the door. The tire swing where she'd spent countless evenings being pushed by her dad was still there, although the rope looked a little frayed. Even though she was a small girl—barely pushing five feet tall, she worried her weight could pull it down.

Stephanie was all breast and ass. Some of her friends had even chided that she looked like a lopsided hourglass, or a cartoon figure. Her breasts came into the room a full five seconds before her, and her ass left five seconds after. It was all an exaggeration, of course, but she did have an amazing body for someone who was so small-statured.

When she entered the house, the smell of disuse was strong in the air. Her mom had spent the final eight months in a nursing home, so the house had been boarded up by a company liaison with hospice. Stephanie insisted on coming in, but the nurses told her there was no use in it. So now, Stephanie made sure the place was at least serviceable for the night—there was running water and electricity. She'd called ahead to make sure those were ready for her when she showed off the house.

She didn't know much about the listing agent, she hadn't even bothered to look at his card. He'd been a referral from the nursing home, and the ladies there spoke so highly of him that Stephanie didn't mind giving him a shot. She had no idea how to list a house, how to have one appraised, or how to find buyers. So if this guy was half as nice as they seemed to think, she'd let him take over the whole show.

The ceilings in her parents' Victorian home were large and vaulted, like a cathedral church. They always seemed massive when she was little, but even now as a grown-up they were imposing. In some places, mainly the foyer and the salon, the ceilings were fifteen feet high. When she came into the kitchen, she was struck by another wave of nostalgia, this one nearly bringing tears to her eyes.

Along the doorframe leading into the hallway was a series of marks, as well as dates. Her dad had measured her height many times, and it was impressive to see how she'd grown over the years. But somewhere around middle school she'd stopped sprouting up, topping out at four feet and eleven inches. Many of these dates she remembered, but several she didn't—it was her dad's fun thing to do.

She put a hand up and felt the smooth, cool wood beneath her palm. The marks were old and faded into the frame, and on a few occasions even carved in. She certainly didn't remember her dad doing that. Her eyes drifted up, and about three feet above her head was a slash across the wood. It must have been a trick of the light, but she was almost sure that it was glowing—a soft red pulse that seemed to disappear the more tried to see it.

Humoring herself, she pressed her back against the doorframe and then pulled out the pen from her inside coat pocket. She traced a line across her head, then stepped away so that she could see the last mark. It was actually an inch or two shorter than her last measurement, all those years back. That thought made her giggle, for it looked like she was shrinking.

However, that wasn't the case at all, for as soon as she separated from the doorframe, an electrical charge passed through her body. She couldn't make sense of it, but it was almost as if her shoes were tighter, and also her sleeves. Stephanie was sweating now—she could feel it running down her back. A part of it was nerves from being here. The memories were all crowding around her, like little hands pulling at her jacket. She needed a hot bath to relax, and was happy to see once she was upstairs that the place was clean—spotless, so she turned on the water and filled the room with steam.

As the mirror started to fog over, she found herself relaxing. Her apartment back home had a very shallow tub, and the one in her mom and dad's master was a clawfoot—very long and very deep. She was able to fill it up to her neck with steaming hot water. And as soon as she was clean, she laid her head back on the rubber pillow and slowly started to drift away. She was feeling good, and subconsciously she dropped a hand down between her legs. However, before she could make any progress with that particular venture, her eyes crept shut and she found herself falling asleep.

When she woke, the water was still hot, so she didn't think she'd been out long, but something felt different. Her feet were resting on the edge of the tub, just past the faucet. But that didn't make sense because for her ankles to be so far up, her head should've been submerged beneath the water, but it didn't feel as though she'd creeped down any at all. Stephanie became alert and she sat up in the tub, splashing water across the floor. Something had definitely changed, and it was making her feel a little worried.

Stephanie stood up and stepped out of the tub, not noticing at first just how easy it had been. She stood in front of the fogged mirror and slid a hand across it, horrified to see her reflection. Before the bath, she'd been in this very spot, observing the gray hairs that were starting to surface along her scalp. When she leaned in, her head came to the top rim of the mirror.

Now, the mirror was angled more with her chest.

"What the fuck?" she said, and the loudness of her voice in the tiny room surprised her.

She took a step back and almost fell into the tub, but quickly caught herself on the shower curtain. Still, her hand grabbed whatever it could, and she pulled the whole thing down, rod and all. Stephanie was definitely bigger. Judging by the doorframe, she guessed she was at least seven feet tall. When she looked down, she made the startling discovery that height wasn't the only thing that had changed.

Her breasts had ballooned out, now like soft melon-sized mounds. She couldn't help but wrap her fingers around them and then gently pull her nipples. They were so much more sensitive now. When she turned sideways to see them in the mirror, she bumped her ass on the edge of the sink, and made the discovery that it too had ballooned out. If she looked like a lopsided hourglass before, she didn't want to think of how it all looked now. Still, she felt positively sexy.

How had this happened? she wondered. She fell asleep in the tub a normal-sized (although small-statured) woman and woke up as an Amazon. She should've been asking a hundred questions but she didn't. This was an awesome development. She was quite glad that it happened. All her life she'd been chastised for being so tiny, and for once she felt beautiful and powerful. If she wanted, she could probably put a fist right through the drywall. Instead, she put on her now very tight-fitting house robe and walked back downstairs.

She ordered a pizza, paying no mind to the guy who didn't seem to even notice she'd barely tipped him, then sat on the sofa and ate in silence. There wasn't much choice, as the cable hadn't been reconnected. But as she was finishing up the last piece of an entire medium pizza, she looked back over to the doorframe and made yet another discovery.

Stephanie put her plate aside and walked over to inspect. There was now a line on the wall, exactly level with her head. When she'd leaned up against it before her bath, that line was a noticeable cut in the wood that, perhaps or perhaps not, held a faint, red glow. But now, a new slash had appeared, and this one was near the top, probably at the twelve-foot mark.

It's showing me, she thought. *It's showing me how big I'll get next time I stand against the door frame.*

A part of her wanted to do just that, for what could be better than being a whopping twelve-foot giantess? But another part, the more grounded, rational part told her to wait. She could always try it out another time, perhaps after the listing agent left. For now, she decided to strip down naked and go to bed. He would be there early the next morning, and it would already be difficult to explain her current size. There weren't many seven-foot-tall women in the world.

***

She woke up the same size, much to her chagrin. Even though she loved being unusually big, it was still an odd thing to happen. What of her health? Her blood pressure, her heart, her brain? Wouldn't those things be adversely affected by gaining another three feet in height? She tried not to think about it, instead did her best to find something to wear. None of her clothes would fit except a tight pair of jogging pants that left her calves exposed, and showed an extreme camel toe between her legs. She wore her bathrobe over top of it.

At a quarter to noon, there was a knock on the door. She'd managed to fix her hair and makeup, but she didn't think the guy would make it any further than her breasts. When she opened the door, a tall man (although not as tall as the Amazon) with a bald head stood on the porch, holding a briefcase. His eyes grew wide as he started at her toes and inspected all the way up to her face. And at the same time, they recognized each other.

"Stephanie?"

"Nick?"

He'd been her BFF all through middle and high school. They went to several dances together. But she wanted out of their town and he didn't, so a part of him resented her for leaving right after graduation. She stopped talking to him and eventually got embarrassed that so much time had passed between them with no communication. It became harder to reach out than ever. She assumed he felt the same way. But now, his smile was genuine, but his eyebrow was arched because he clearly saw the difference from the last time they'd been next to one another.

"You look . . . different," he said.

"Do I?" she asked, playing dumb.

"Uh, yeah. You were like right here the last time we talked." He brought a hand up to his chest. Nick was a tall guy, almost six feet tall, and she'd spent her whole life looking up to him. This was a rather nice change and she wasn't about to lose this momentum.

"I guess I had a growth spurt," she said. "C'mon in." She backed away from the door, careful not to turn away because she wasn't so sure how her ass was looking in such a tight, makeshift getup.

He came in and placed his briefcase on the coffee table. "I'm sorry to hear about your mom. She was a great lady. I can always remember trick-or-treating here when we were little. She always gave us the good stuff."

"Snickers," said Stephanie.

"Snickers," said Nick, breathing a sigh of reminiscence. And then, shaking from his reverie, he said, "I guess I should go over a few things." Then, he was opening his briefcase so he could fish out several important-looking documents.

But his eyes kept glancing up at her as she sat on the edge of the sofa, her body ready to explode from the tight-fitting clothes. In that moment she could see the lust in his eyes, and she felt it too. They'd never so much as touched, but there had been a few innocent kisses back when they were still in school. Neither of them ever wanted to pursue a romantic relationship, but it had been two years since she'd last touched a guy. And Nick was looking positively gorgeous right now in his three-piece suit.

"You okay?" she asked him as he stumbled over his words twice. He laughed and dropped his head, face turning red.

"Yeah," he said, and without looking up he pointed to her and said, "I just wasn't expecting all this."

She sat up straight and pulled her robe a little looser. "But is it a bad thing?" she asked, biting her fingernail.

He grinned and shook his head. He looked like he was going to pass out.

"That suit looks awfully hot. And that tie looks uncomfortable. Feel free to lose the jacket."

He nodded, seeing no harm in doing as she said and removed his jacket, then balled his tie up and unfastened the top button of his shirt. He fanned himself with his collar and then tried once again to get started. Stephanie simply glided over to the spot on the sofa right next to him and pretended to peer down at the paperwork. In truth, her breasts were blocking her from seeing anything directly below her. Nick was still smiling, still sweating. He wouldn't even dare a look at her now, just continued to mumble his words.

She knew she had to be the one to make the first move.

Her hand crept across his thigh, and he immediately tensed up. But after that, he relaxed and she took that to mean that he was accepting of her forwardness. There were no more words, as she put a hand to his cheek and pulled him around so that she could kiss him. His lips were so soft, but he was shy and didn't participate much until her hand moved north and started to stroke between his legs.

That ignited a fire in him, and the moment she moved her hand away, he was on top of her, but it was rather comical because he was now smaller. Nick was a strong guy, but she was currently stronger. She maneuvered him between her legs, then wrapped them around his body and pushed him forward. That's when she heard the tight jogging pants start to rip along her ankles, to which he looked down and laughed.

"This isn't normal for you, is it?" he asked, coming in to kiss her along the neck. "This size, I mean."

"Maybe not, but let's just go with it, okay?"

He was eager to agree, and both started to pull off the other's clothes. She was delighted to see such a firm chest, and he was thrilled when she finally peeled off the tight housecoat and let her breasts bounce uninhibited. Nick was quick to raise one up so he could pop a nipple into his mouth. It felt incredible—the first touch of a man in so long, and it was already making her weak in the knees and wet between the legs.

When he stood up between her legs to take his pants off, she decided he was dawdling too long, so she ripped his belt through the loops and then pulled his slacks down. He had a raging hard-on beneath his underwear, and the tip was already wet from his pre-cum. She leaned in and kissed his stomach, and could feel his muscles tighten with each touch. Then, using her oversized fingers, she pulled his underwear down, and was delighted to see just how thick his cock appeared. She couldn't help but give it a few test strokes, squeezing out a little more pre-cum.

"He's a big boy," said Stephanie.

"Are you sure?" Nick asked. "You're a big lady."

"I'm sure he'll be fine."

She put him in her mouth, to which his hands rested gently in her hair. His whole body relaxed, legs barely keeping him upright. Stephanie didn't know if she was good in bed or not, but she did know she was good at sucking dick. It was a personal goal for how quickly she could get a man off. And now, having a much larger mouth—with larger lips and tongue, she figured she had the potential to be a master. With the way Nick's eyes were rolling back into his head, she figured she was doing a good job. But she didn't want to get him off. If he were lucky, they would circle back to this.

Before he could blow up in her mouth, she pulled her lips away and then leaned back on the sofa. She put her legs in the air while he got down on his knees, then threw them over his shoulders.

"Careful there, big girl," he said, bracing himself on the sofa. She didn't pay him any attention, only continued to use her weight and force to drive his face toward her pussy. He buried himself between her legs, and now she was the one worried about getting off too quickly. But that was the beauty of being a girl—it wasn't a one-shot and then done. Ladies could go all night if they had the right guy. And right now, she was sure she had the right guy. She closed her eyes and let him eat.

When it was time to get started, she lifted him up, mouth dripping, and helped guide his dick into her waiting pussy. He was big enough (or perhaps she was small enough) that it felt amazing. He cupped his hands on her breasts and started to stroke. He was effective at sex, but this wasn't the right place for it. She wanted a bed, she wanted to be able to stretch out and feel every inch of him, so she pushed him away, to which he gave her an odd look.

"Let's go upstairs," she said, standing in all her naked glory.

"Sounds good," he agreed, and they started kissing again before they'd even moved an inch. He pushed her against the wall and went down on her again, she pushed him against another wall and did the same. They slowly made their way up the steps, half-fucking, half-walking. By the time they made it to the bed, he was on top of her, easing his massive cock back inside her.

He was able to get her off several times, and because her skin already felt electrified, because her body already felt numb and warm, she didn't notice the subtle change at first. It was Nick who made the discovery.

"I'm . . . slipping out," he said. He was constantly having to reposition his dick inside her. "It's like . . . oh, holy fuck!"

"What?" she said, sitting up and pushing him off her, but that was all she needed to know exactly what had alarmed him.

Her feet and ankles were disappearing over the edge of the bed. He was on his knees, just between them, and it looked as if his whole body was shrinking, but that wasn't the case at all. Stephanie had started to grow again, and it didn't take a rocket scientist to understand why.

During their aggressive kissing on the way up to the bedroom, they'd rolled around along the wall—and he'd pushed her right up against the magic doorframe. Now, she was climbing to match the height of the newest slash— twelve feet.

"This is bad," said Nick. "Isn't it?"

"Not at all. Get back here." She pulled him back down and shoved his face right against her waiting pussy, which was stretching long and wide against his head. He went back to work, dutifully flicking his tongue in and out, and running it along her lips. Nick mouthed her clit, to which she almost immediately got off, squirting him right in the face. Still, she continued to grow, her weight causing the feeble bed to bow in the middle.

She became even more aggressive, to the point that he was making little cries. Her fingers, while still growing, ran through his hair and grabbed. It was such a rush to be in charge of him, to control where his face went. If she wasn't careful, she'd get drunk on this power, for who could stop a twelve-foot giantess?

They moved off the bed, mainly to confirm that she was a twelve-foot giantess, and she pressed him against the wall. She got down on her knees and pinned him with her abnormally large breasts. Now, he had trouble fitting her nipple in his mouth. It was such a turn on to watch him struggle, to see him almost gag because it filled his mouth so much.

He loved her ass, and couldn't keep his hands off it. She leaned against the wall, placing her large palms flat, and pushed it out so he could see it and play with it. Nick found his own aggression, slapping it over and over just to watch how much it jiggled. It felt good, and each time his hand connected, a warm tingle ran the course of her body.

After she'd been serviced enough, she got down on her knees and finished the job that she'd started downstairs. Now, his dick was hardly big enough to make her gag. The main problem was keeping it in the center of her mouth so that she didn't accidentally bite it. But she found a good rhythm and started to suck. He was tensing up, most likely fearful to look down and see nothing but a giant head of hair. But she pushed him back gently on the bed, making him lie flat, and then she was able to bob up and down more effectively. It didn't take long for his tiny, miniscule load to warm her tongue.

After it was over, he just stared down at her while she sat on her knees.

"What the hell happened, Steph? You're so big!" He brought a hand down to stroke her shoulder, as if he were just now seeing her again for the first time.

"It was . . . I don't know what it was," she said honestly. "There's a doorframe downstairs where my dad recorded my height as I grew up. And I put my back to it—twice, and each time I got bigger and bigger."

"So it was your dad's doing? Like, is he a wizard or something?"

She giggled at that. "No, I don't think so. But it *is* magic, I think. My parents probably didn't even realize it."

"You should pry off that board when you leave here," he said. "Take the growing magic with you."

"That's not such a bad idea," she said, and then joined him on the bed.

They talked all evening, ate another pizza (to which Nick answered the door this time) and then fell asleep upstairs on the bed, her long legs hanging over. She had dreams the entire night of being gigantic—her huge feet stomping tiny cities, and of the military firing missiles at her huge breasts. But sometime during the night, Nick slipped away, and it wouldn't be until morning when she found him.

***

When she woke up the next morning, Nick was gone. Her first thought was that he freaked out after giving it some thought, and left without telling her. But when she rolled over (still twelve-foot tall) and looked out the window, she saw his car still sitting in the driveway. Perhaps he decided to fix breakfast, or perhaps he just needed some alone time.

She stood up, amazed by how much the house had changed. It was odd looking at the tops of doors, at the dusty tops of shelves. Things along the ground seemed so far away now. Whenever she took a step, the whole place shook. The picture frames rattled on the wall. Her massive footsteps were the only things she heard throughout the whole house as she trudged down the steps.

Her hands graced the walls and she looked at the world through new eyes. She gazed over at the wall that made it all possible, and wondered what would happen if she squeezed against it one more time. But that was a fleeting thought because from here she could see into most of the rooms, and Nick was nowhere to be found.

"Nick?" she called out, stepping into the living room. It was silent, but she heard something far off, or perhaps muted, like music from headphones. She looked around and took another few steps toward the sofa, marveling by how the furniture looked like dollhouse goods.

But then, she heard Nick—and he was screaming. She stepped into the kitchen, but the noise was coming from behind her. She whipped around, looked down at the sofa—and there stood Nick.

Only now, he was just a foot tall. He was trying to get her attention and he was completely naked. His little dick was bobbing up and down as he jumped and waved his hands. It would have been cute if it hadn't been so alarming.

"Nick? What did you do?" But she already knew the answer.

"I wanted . . . I wanted to get big," he said. "Fuck you with a giant cock, you know? But when I stood against the doorframe . . . I didn't grow."

"Seems to affect men and women different. That's my guess. Wow, you're so tiny!" She brought up a finger and tapped him in the chest.

When she stood up to her full height, she was certain that he couldn't see her face any longer, for the sofa—and the little man on it—had disappeared on the other side of her breasts. He had gone quiet for a moment, most likely staring at her gorgeous body. She was so massive now, and although he was a foot tall, her being twelve feet high made him seem like a six-inch man.

"I think we should call someone," he said, panic in his voice. "This isn't normal. It's one thing for you to be so big, but me . . . I'm tiny!"

"You are," she said. "And I think it's kind of hot."

"You do?" he asked. She got down on the floor, for the sofa would probably crumble under her weight.

"Oh yes." She scooped him up and placed him on the floor between her legs. "Because now, I think you're just the right size for an idea I have."

He looked dead ahead, to the massive pussy that was, coincidentally, just big enough to swallow him whole.

"You want me . . ." His voice trailed off and he pointed ahead.

"Yep. Get to it, little man."

She rocked her legs out, arched her back, and used her hands against her knees to keep herself open.

His little hands felt amazing and it surprised her that someone so small could be so effective. It didn't matter that his dick had been reduced to the size of a broken toothpick.

Now, his whole body was the best dick in the world. He was forceful again, pushing his arms and face into her until she relaxed enough to let him pass. Stephanie struggled to keep herself on the floor, to keep her arms and legs from flailing out and destroying her parents' house. After all, he was eventually going to help her sell it.

But right now it was as if he were doing jumping jacks inside her pussy, his arms and legs moving to great effect. She didn't want to cum—she wanted to ride the edge for as long as she could but the very thought that there was a tiny man inside her made her lose control. Her whole body relaxed, then went rigid, then relaxed again. She was comforted each time she felt him moving because it was a real fear of hers that she would crush him or drown him. But Nick could take care of himself, and once it was over, he slid himself out and landed in a wet puddle between her legs. He ran a hand over his slick, bald head, and stared up at her, hand on hip.

"It's almost like you've done that before!" she said, breathing heavily. He shrugged, as if perhaps he had.

"I enjoyed that immensely. But we need to try to understand the magic here."

"I agree." She stood up and placed the tiny man on the counter in the kitchen.

Then, using her bare fingers, she ripped the doorframe right off the wall and placed it on the sofa.

"Okay," she said. "I suppose I'm ready to sell the house now."

The
Rise of Venus

Venus's parents had high hopes when they named her. The name evoked stature—power, nobility, and as of late, a star tennis player. But she was certainly a disappointment because Venus wasn't any of those things. She was an overworked, four-foot-eleven weakling. She was pale, had no breasts or ass and would've been considered quite ordinary if not for her pretty face. Freckles covered her nose and cheeks, and her mop of red hair hung down past her shoulders. She was a hit with the guys, at least in the beginning and only because she was needy. Once they got what they wanted, she never heard from them again.

She and Nick had been dating for almost a year now, and things were going well, but she never understood what he saw in her. Surely a guy as tall and good-looking as Nick would have options—options that didn't include a minuscule sprite like Venus. He took good care of her, paid for everything, and even floated her a few dollars to make her rent when her hours were cut at her restaurant. Nick was generally just a good guy.

They were having dinner on the night when everything started to change.

He invited her out to El Patio's, her favorite Mexican place in town. It was summer, and the place was packed with young and old. There'd been a new action-thriller to play at the cinema down the street, and all those moviegoers were now crowding inside, waiting to find a table.

"We got here just in time," she said, just as they sat down. Their waiter took their drink order and left the menus.

"We did," said Nick, looking at the long line of people standing by the counter. He seemed preoccupied, although she couldn't put her finger on it. Nick worked for a construction company but he didn't necessarily get his hands dirty. He spent all day in an office overlooking the worksite, filling out invoices and purchase orders. Although it wasn't stressful, he still had a lot people depending on him. So Venus usually allowed him to have his little quiet spells.

As they ordered their food and began making small-talk she realized it wasn't because of any of these things that kept him quiet. Nick had beautiful eyes, and she often stared, and that's how she knew he was tracking someone moving about the restaurant behind her.

"So I'd hoped we could talk about the place over on Lindhurst Avenue," she said just after their food arrived. "I could have my stuff packed in two days if it's still available."

"Yeah, sure," he said, taking a drink of Coke, his eyes fixated on something behind Venus.

"They need first- and last-month's rent, but that's normal. Can you be out of your place by the seventh?"

It had taken so long to convince him to get an apartment with her. If this relationship was moving toward a family, then this was the next logical step. Neither of them was ready to get married, certainly not ready for a baby, but having a place together just seemed right. At least in her eyes.

"Um . . ." He took another swig of Coke and followed someone behind Venus once more, his train of thought dissolving.

"Do you see something you like, Nick?" she asked. When he didn't respond, she hit the table with her open palm hard enough that a few people seated nearby stopped eating and looked over. Nick stared at her as if her head had floated away.

"What?"

"I'm trying to have a serious conversation with you and you won't stop looking at someone."

"What? You're being silly."

Venus could feel her face growing warm. She hated being talked down to—especially if it implied that she was being child-like. She had enough hang-ups when it came to her small stature, and she surely wasn't going to tolerate them from her boyfriend.

"I'm not being silly. Who is it?" Venus whipped her head around just in time to see the waitress walk by.

It was a tall, leggy Latino girl but the only thing Venus noticed was the way her shirt was unbuttoned, and how her large breasts were spilling out. She was easily in a double-D, and each step she took made them bounce. After she'd passed the table, Venus saw that her ass was just as impressive, thick and bulbous. The girl was simply perfection, and she couldn't really blame Nick for looking, but Venus *could* blame him for the way she was being ignored.

The worst part was how he continued to watch her even though Venus had made it quite clear she was upset. She leaned back in her chair and folded her arms over and crossed her legs. Nick was still watching her talk to customers across the room, and he was probably jealous he and Venus hadn't been seated in her section.

"What?" Nick asked finally, once the waitress had passed behind Venus and he saw just how intently her eyes were fixed on him.

"Is that what you want?" she asked. "You're eye-fucking her hard enough."

"What are you talking about?" he said, and it was clear he genuinely didn't know. That's how rapt he'd been in the waitress's presence. And knowing that hurt Venus even more.

"Nevermind. You know what? I'm going to go. If you want a girl with massive tits, you picked the wrong one."

Venus fished a wad of cash out of her purse and dropped it on the table, then stood up and stormed out. Nick was chasing her, his voice just loud enough for her to hear because he didn't want to cause a scene. But she was a fast walker on her short legs and managed to pull away from him. She flashed a look from the corner of her eye and saw a waiter carrying a tray of steaming food had stepped into his path, and that put even more distance between him and the fleeing woman.

She stepped out into cool air and darted into a waiting cab. By the time it pulled away, Nick wasn't even out of the restaurant yet. Sitting in the backseat, Venus had tears in her eyes. This had probably been an overreaction, but she didn't care. It had been during a moment when she'd poured her heart out, and it was an embarrassment for him to be checking out another woman—especially one so different, so attractive and well-built.

The cab let her out at her apartment, but just before she could dart up the steps, a brilliant light caught her attention. She looked up, and there in the sky was a thin line skating across, heading right toward the mountains. And then, a loud boom. Whatever it was . . . it was close. Although she wanted nothing more than to get inside, take a shower and go to bed, she decided to investigate the woods.

Just beyond the treeline, she saw an orange glow—fire. She crouched down, hopeful to see something in the crash site, and that's when her phone began to buzz, startling her so badly that she dropped it and then had to fish around in the dirt until she could find it. Naturally, it was Nick. A part of her wanted to send it straight to voicemail, but another part said she needed to answer it. They never went to bed angry, and she didn't want to start tonight.

"What?" she asked, still moving through the forest, her feet crunching on leaves.

"Are you okay?" he said. She had expected him to get mad and yell at her, as most guys did once you called them on their bad behavior. But his voice was calm and gentle.

"Yeah," she said. "Just . . . pissed."

"I'm sorry," he said. "I shouldn't have been staring that way. You're twice as gorgeous as that girl."

Venus rolled her eyes. "As if."

"Really. I shouldn't be checking out other girls. I should only be checking out you."

"It's fine, Nick. Really. I know I don't have much going on, and I guess I have to be okay with that. Listen, I'm going to bed, so we'll talk tomorrow."

He was quiet for a moment, as if he didn't know how to proceed, but thankfully he took the easy way out and simply said, "Okay. Goodnight and I love you. I'll see you in the morning."

"I love you, too," she said, and hung up.

She was almost near the fire now, and once she was standing over it, she realized it was a metal capsule—not a meteorite like she'd originally thought. This thing was like a small tube, but broken in the middle. There was something inside it that was catching the light from the fire, so she used her foot to move the capsule halves aside. There on the ground lay a pendant—a beautiful necklace with a little emerald in the center. Venus couldn't believe her eyes.

She reached down and picked it up, loving the weight of its chain between her fingers. The star-filled sky above had sent it to her, she was sure. It was a silly notion but she couldn't explain it any better. The designs on the pendant looked Greek, and she would've probably been better off taking it to a university, to some expert in Latin, but she didn't want to part with it. Venus balled up the chain and shoved it into her pocket, then headed back toward her apartment building.

Once inside, she fed her guinea pig then hopped in the shower. After tonight, she hated looking in the full-length bathroom mirror. It was depressing to see such a flat chest, knowing that there were other women out there— like the waitress—who had so much more. Venus had large nipples, but it didn't matter since they stood at the end of such flat mounds. It was making her feel bad about herself, so she got dressed and went to bed.

Right before she fell asleep, a green light shone through her eyelids. She opened her eyes but didn't see anything. Venus got up to use the bathroom but before returning to bed she looked over at the pendant sprawled across her dresser. It was cool to the touch, almost like silk. As it dangled on its golden chain, collecting glints of the streetlight out the window, she was filled with a sense of calm. For reasons she couldn't comprehend, she slipped it over her neck. There were no breasts for it to settle between, but that was okay. It still felt nice against her skin.

She went back to sleep, her fingers gently caressing the smooth stone.

***

Venus overslept, so she completely forgot about having breakfast with Nick that morning. It wasn't until she heard a heavy knock on her door that she stirred. It was the knock of someone who'd been there a few minutes already, and was growing worried or impatient. She hopped out of bed and looked at her phone to see she had six missed text messages from him. By this point, he probably thought something was wrong, that she'd slipped and fell overnight, and was currently lying facedown in a pool of her own blood.

She hopped up and ran to the door, too intent to open it to notice how her gravity had changed, how the dimensions of her body were different. Venus looked through the keyhole to confirm it was Nick, then pulled the door open.

"You okay?" he said, and then, "Holy hell!" His eyes had moved down to her chest.

She followed his gaze and took a step back, figuring there was a spider crawling across her t-shirt, but that wasn't the case at all. Venus couldn't even see her feet because the shirt was so puffed out. And it was so puffed out because she now had enormous breasts. As she became aware of them, they tingled, and then the nipples began to harden. They poked through, like tiny daggers.

"Shit," she said, rubbing her palms across them through the shirt. "This is . . . really cool."

"Cool? What the hell happened, Venus?" She was backing away and he was entering the apartment.

"Shut the door," she said. "And come in here."

When she got back into the bedroom, she didn't even notice that Chuck, her guinea pig, was missing. She sat down on the bed and pulled off her shirt, letting her giant breasts bounce, her red hair falling across them. Nick walked into the room with his mouth open, unsure of what to say or do. He was panicked, and Venus probably should've been as well, but this was a good turn of events for someone who'd been small-chested her whole life.

"You're being far too calm for me. Aren't you freaking out? You grew breasts overnight!"

"I would think this would be a good thing for you," she said, massaging her nipples. She crossed her legs over, feeling a tingle run the course of her body. She was certainly more sensitive this morning than she had been last night.

"Oh hush," he said. "You need to let last night go, Venus. I'm sorry about that, okay?"

She just stared at him and leaned back, and then, before the conversation could become heated, she decided to diffuse it. "Come here."

"What?"

"Come here. Touch them. I know you want to."

He stood in place for a moment, as if gauging her reaction. She'd changed gears so fast that he thought it was a trap, that if he did as she asked, it was only confirming that this was all he wanted. She was gorgeous there on the bed, wearing a sheer pair of panties and nothing else. Her toes were painted pink, and she was clenching them, as she often did when she was excited. Right now, she was being honest—and she wanted him to put his hands on her.

Nick sat on the bed next to her and rubbed his palm against the soft mound of flesh. She was warm and she shuddered a little at his touch. He massaged them for only a few seconds before hooking his hand down and taking her nipple between his fingers. Even those had grown—and as he played, they became more erect. The areolas were like dark, saucer-sized circles. Venus was biting her bottom lip, as if she were fighting the urge to get worked up. It was failing, because as his hands caressed her slopes, she felt another tingle, and knew she was wet between the legs.

"Suck on them," she said, and lay back on the bed. They were so large that they almost fell to the sides, but she kept her hands against them for support, and as they were squeezed they looked even bigger.

He began by running his fingers up and down her thigh. Venus loved that, and she immediately broke out in goosebumps which always made her giggle. His hand moved to her stomach where he traced a line across her bellybutton before moving south, inside the panties. Her heat and wetness were clear, and as he plunged his fingers into her sweet spot, her own fingers came up and started to tweak her nipples.

"Where did you get that?" he asked, fingers working. He nodded toward the pendant which had been consumed between her breasts.

And that's when it all became clear—she'd been given this pendant as a way to better herself, as a way to get the breasts she'd always wanted. She didn't know if it was God, fate, or something else, but it was obvious something was helping her inadequacies. With Nick's fingers inside her, she was starting to gain a little confidence.

"I found it last night," she said. "I think it's what made my body change."

"That's crazy," he said, continuing to finger.

"Is it? It's no crazier than waking up with a pair of monstrous breasts," she said.

"Touché."

Nick leaned down and popped a nipple into his mouth. It was so large, like sucking on a soda bottle, but each tug made her moan. Venus put her hands against his bald head, and that pulled him closer. He abandoned her pussy for the moment and used all of his fingers to squeeze her breasts. His tongue darted out, doing little circles around her nipple that made her writhe on the bed. One hand reached back and clenched the sheet. She'd never gotten off from someone playing with her nipple, but in that moment she thought she could.

He switched breasts, and now he was lying across her, his large frame holding her down, dominating her. She stroked his head and gently pushed him forward, wanting him to be a little more aggressive but also not wanting to say it. She didn't understand how the necklace was changing her so. She was feeling . . . better—better about herself and better about her relationship. Just as her breasts had grown, so too had her confidence.

Her whole body was warm, but as he played, she couldn't escape the fact that the pendant had also heated. It was supernatural because Nick didn't seem to notice. He moved aside, and pulled her panties completely off and began going down on her, occasionally reaching up and tweaking her breast. Venus put her arms above her head, spread her legs and let her man eat. It was the best feeling in the world, and was somehow different than it had been before. The pendant had changed so much.

But the pendant was just getting started.

Nick climbed atop her, pushing his dick inside. She made a soft moan and pulled him down by the neck. It was a little awkward with the breasts because she wasn't used to having him squash them in order to get a kiss. Still, it wasn't a detraction. They made out just as hard, and he fucked her just as aggressively as ever. When he threw her legs up over his shoulders, she began to notice yet another change.

She'd become super aware of her new breasts, and that's how she determined that they were growing again. Nick dropped one of her legs and started sucking on her left nipple, and it was as if his head kept getting smaller with each tug of his mouth. Her legs were stretching out across the bed, but surely that was an illusion. Nick's weight lessened, and that's when she realized it wasn't in her head—that she was actually getting larger in addition to her breasts. He seemed to notice it too, because he lifted himself off the bed, and he barely had enough room to clear his face of her boobs.

"Shit, Venus. What's happening? You're . . . bigger! Not just your boobs. It's all bigger!"

He stood up, suddenly fearful. And when his body had moved away from her, she looked down at the length of the bed and saw just how her heels were touching the footboard. Even then, her knees had to bend slightly. The bed was six feet long, so that meant . . .

"I'm like seven feet tall!" she said, and stood up next to the now much smaller man. He was barely coming up to her breasts now.

"I don't think . . . I don't think that's all that happened," he said, looking at his hands and turning them over to see the backs.

"What do you mean?" she asked, but as he put his back near her dresser, she figured it out quite quickly.

Nick often leaned down to feed her guinea pig, whose cage was situated on top of her dresser. But seeing him stand in front of it, she could tell that he would never be able to do it now. Just like Venus until recently, Nick would need to stand on her stepladder to even reach Chuck's water bottle. There had been an exchange of size, of that she had no doubt.

"You're smaller," she said.

"Yeah. You shrunk me!"

"Me? What did *I* do?"

"It's clear, Venus. You got bigger at the same moment I got smaller. You stole my inches!"

There was no other way to explain it, and as she looked over his head and into Chuck's cage, she realized she'd taken her pet's size too—last night she'd exchanged her guinea pig's size for a new set of breasts. Strangely, she didn't feel bad or sorry for any of this.

"Well, what do you think of me?" she asked him, stepping back toward the doorway so he could see her. She couldn't see his face because her breasts were so large. "Not bad, huh?"

"I don't understand how you can remain so calm. Doesn't this scare you?"

She shook her head. "It may even be temporary, who knows? But I'm enjoying this. And I think I could make you enjoy it too."

She put her hands on his arms and moved him over to the bed, then kissed down his stomach until she reached his dick. He'd already started to go soft from the panic, but she remedied that rather quickly with a few well-placed kisses along his shaft. Nick sounded as though he were trying to stifle his own moans, but she rubbed a large hand up his stomach and began sucking him, something that was far easier now that there was such a size-difference in her mouth and his dick.

It never took him long to shoot his load when it was in her mouth, and with the added stimuli of her being so large and having a more powerful tongue, he was done in under two minutes. After she swallowed him, she moved up the bed, her large arms holding her breasts up high enough for him to suck. The pendant was cool again, and it dragged along the shrunken man's stomach.

"Suck," she ordered, staring at the headboard. No more could she see the tiny man under her, but she could certainly feel him as he went to work. The sensitivity only increased the bigger she got, and already she could feel her cum trickling down her thighs. Nick did as she asked, switching between nipples and leaving them painfully hard in the process.

And that's when she felt the pendant become warm again.

Venus had no control over its power, and even if she did, she wasn't so sure she would *want* to control it. But as she lay there on top of Nick, she felt her breasts ballooning out, and they became so large and round that he had to use all his might to push up, or else he'd be suffocated beneath them. She giggled at the thought of seeing a coroner's report. But when she was on her haunches, she could see the panic in his face. So far, only her breasts were growing.

"Maybe a little left over power from before?" she asked, tweaking them. Nick didn't respond, only leaned in and popped her nipple into his mouth again. Her breasts were comically large now, and she wasn't even sure there was a scale to measure them, unless 'needing-a-wheelbarrow' was a size.

But then, they both shuddered with a warm tingle. Venus began to grow again, at just the same time Nick started to shrink.

"Fuck!" he said, hopping off the bed. "How small now?"

"Stay on the bed, sweetheart," said Venus. "Or else you might not be able to climb back up." He seemed put off by these words, but nonetheless, he did as she asked and climbed back, sitting at the headboard. His body continued to close up, head moving down, feet moving back. His raging hard-on never left.

By the time it was over, Venus could feel the bed starting to buckle with her weight. Since she was on the footboard end, the bottom legs snapped and she was left with a bed that sloped. Nick struggled to keep his balance—he looked absolutely miniscule now. He was scared, but she couldn't relate. She'd never felt more powerful and beautiful in her life.

"What's wrong, shrimp?" she said. "Not enjoying this ride anymore?"

"It's freaking me out, Venus! Look at us!"

"Stand up, shorty, and I will."

She got up and nearly bumped her head on the ceiling. From the architectural plans, she knew that the ceilings were twelve-feet tall, and now so was she. Nick stood on the bed, and even with its added height, he didn't come up to her crotch. He was probably less than two feet tall now.

"I bet you really like these girls now, huh?" she said, sitting on the floor and playing with her breasts. He didn't know what to say, so she grabbed him by the legs and put him there on her chest, upside down. Holding his legs, she began licking his cock, right when he latched onto her nipple and started to kiss along it. She didn't think he could pop the whole thing in his mouth any longer. As he was working, she looked down and noticed the cool pendant—it had scaled with her body, and was now much larger, looking like a little shield next to her tiny boyfriend.

She loved this size difference, and so did he, apparently. Once she was done with that, she put him in the floor where he completely disappeared from her sight. She leaned back, spreading all across her bedroom floor, and let him use his legs and arms to get her off. Nick's little hands were squeezing her clit, and each time she felt it, a shiver ran down her spine. Was it the arousal that made them change sizes? She wasn't sure, but either way, it was about to happen again.

"No, no, no!" said Nick, standing up. He must have felt the same tingle in his body that she felt in hers.

"Quick, climb up!" she said, holding him with two hands and placing his mouth and arms directly in front of her breast. Nick started to kiss it, to massage it. His little tongue was licking it all over, and just like that, she shuddered and they began to change size once again.

Now, she was worried that she would run out of room. Or, worse than that, become so heavy that she collapsed through the floor. That would certainly be a conversation piece with the downstairs neighbors. Venus could feel Nick shrinking in her hands, as if she were holding nothing more than sand. Her breasts were so large, so all-encompassing, that she had to rely completely on feeling and not at all on sight.

He was saying something, but she couldn't understand, nor was she really listening. She was trying to keep from wrecking her apartment, which was a challenge in itself. She maneuvered around so that she was sitting against her closet doors, and that way her feet could grow straight out the door, and into the hallway that led to the kitchen. Looking up, the ceiling was coming dangerously close, but she didn't think it would be a problem as long as her growing soon came to a close. Nick went from being clutched in her hand, to sitting on it, and even now he was still growing smaller.

When she was satisfied that their changing had stopped, she brought Nick up from beneath her breast and looked at him. It almost took her breath away to see him so small, like an inch-sized man, although she was sure he was bigger than that. With her constant growth, they were splitting the difference.

Venus angled herself so that her knees could hold her breasts up, pushing her nipples more upright. Then, she dropped the tiny man onto her areola, his weight barely noticeable. He put a hand next to her nipple and rubbed, and already it was growing taller than his whole body. She thought he'd be mad, but the way his dick stretched, she was sure that he would forgive her.

"Any idea how big you are?" he asked, although he had to yell it so she could hear him.

"Judging by the size of my feet through the doorway, I'm guessing twenty-five feet."

"Holy shit," he said, running his hands atop his head. "This is bad, Venus."

"Nonsense, little man. Your goddess desires pleasure. Now get to it."

He stared at her for a moment, as if trying to gauge how she'd said it—whether she was being silly or not. But either way, he leaned in, wrapped her nipple in a full-body hug and started to kiss it. Just seeing her tiny man perched there on her nipple was enough to make her wet all over again. Her nipples started to stand up, and he lost his hold, unable to accommodate how they'd widened. And then, they were growing taller, passing up his entire body. Once, Nick was a six-foot tall man, and now he had to look up to see the ends of her nipples.

She pressed her breasts together tightly and let him walk from one to the other, almost tumbling down the gap between them. When he was on his feet again, it took all of his might to climb the next one. It was enjoyable to watch him, and a part of her loved having this power—the power to do anything she wanted. In her mind, she saw herself running the country, the world. Growing bigger and bigger and bigger until her feet covered whole cities.

Venus shook herself from the daydream and watched her man play, servicing her other nipple with just as much effort. It had to be tiring, but she loved it. For the final act, she took him on the tip of her finger, then reached below and shoved him right into her pussy. He seemed unwilling, but he didn't have much choice. When you were so small, you listened to your master.

He barely made ripples inside her, except when his body bumped up against the walls of her pussy, but even then it was muted because he was so tiny. If only he were around six or seven inches, then he would feel nice. But she let him swim in her juices for a few moments before returning him to her nipple.

"This was nice, wasn't it?" she said, voice booming.

"It was. But it's scary," he said.

"You shouldn't be scared. I'll take care of you," she said.

"How?"

"You let me worry about that," she said. "All I ask is that you bow down before your goddess."

He looked at her as if she were joking. And then, they both felt the warm tingle. His eyes looked as though they might well with tears. She threw her head back and laughed.

"Bow down and worship while you still have the chance, little man."